LAST THINGS

by

Wm Kane

SHIVA'S KARMA LLC

This book is dedicated to my Beloved FireBird,

Whose support and belief in my creative endeavors has been beyond measure.

TABLE OF CONTENTS

1 – A SNIFFER'S TALE

Joey Adebayo bolted upright, swinging his legs to the side of the bed, his hands clutching his head, which was exploding in spasms of intense pain, from the top of his crown to the nape of his neck. It was so sharp he nearly bit the tip of his tongue off, which made him cry out loudly in severe pain. He covered his mouth to muffle his scream and glanced quickly at the still sleeping form of his wife, Carmen. She rustled herself briefly and without waking up from a languid slumber, nestled her face deeper into the down pillow pressed tightly to her cheek. "Sweet dreams, my love," Joey mouthed silently in her direction as he gazed at his dear, long-suffering wife, who had to put up with his mysterious moods and ailments without really knowing what was wrong or why the "doctors" he was always in consultation with couldn't cure him. Moreover, she was still a little embarrassed when trying to explain to her girlfriends how it was that Joey made money as 'some kind of medical guinea pig.' Joey shook his head slowly in commiseration and let out a long, deep sigh. He just didn't have the heart to tell her the real story.

"Damn," Joey thought to himself as yet another sharp bolt of pain dug deep into the middle of his forehead, "this must be some really big shit." He got up from the bed, still holding his throbbing head, and tried to quietly pick through the pile of clothes on the floor near his closet to find his bathrobe in the pitch blackness of the room. Failing after several attempts which only resulted in a few scraped knuckles and a well-stubbed toe, he shrugged his shoulders and resigned himself to facing the morning chill in the nude as he made his way out of the bedroom and down the hall. The door to little Jerrold's room was ajar and Joey took a quick peek inside to see his son's angelic face fast adrift in the land of winkin', blinkin' and nod, sucking on his thumb and gurgling contentedly to himself. "Just like his mother," Joey thought. He gingerly brushed the tips of his fingers against his throbbing temples, which exploded in another severe spasm of pain that caused him to slump to his knees in the hallway as he closed the door to Jerrold's room.

Across the hall was his daughter Candice's room, but Joey didn't dare to open the door, since like her father Candice was a light sleeper. Even at the tender age of four Candice was already exhibiting the unique traits that made Joey so extraordinary. She could "see" events long before they actually happened, like when she came into the kitchen one day and announced to Carmen that Nana, Joey's mother, had fallen down the stairs and needed an ambulance, even though her beloved Nana was on the phone with her daughter-in-law at that very moment. Three months later, Nana did indeed suffer a bad fall exactly as Candice had described, down to the exact time of day and circumstances. To this day, Nana calls

Candice her little guardian angel and often asks what she sees happening next for her grandmother.

And just last year, around Christmas, Candice surprised even Joey. While out shopping for presents with her father, Candice insisted on having a particular toy, but Joey and Carmen had already decided that that toy would be better suited for Candice when she was a little older. When Joey told Candice she couldn't have the toy just then, she didn't pout or make a scene; she just folded her hands across her chest and followed Joey out of the toy store. When they finally got to where their car was in the parking garage, Joey was shocked to find the whole car covered with the very toy that Candice insisted on getting. It seems that she had telekinesis as well. Joey explained to Candice that it wasn't right for her to take all of the toys and she should put them back for other little boys and girls to have as presents too. Though at first reluctant, Candice agreed and sent the toys flying back to the store just the way they had come. Joey promised to give her a special surprise and asked her to keep the whole affair a secret just between the two of them. Sharing a secret with daddy was much better than any old toy in Candice's view and she readily became a co-conspirator of Joey's. Between jolts of pain, Joey sensed beyond the door and felt the familiar radiance of his daughter fast asleep on the other side, and smiled as he padded down the stairs into the foyer.

Buddy, the family Labrador and real master of the house, roused himself with a shake from under the dining room table and groggily hobbled over to Joey on unsteady legs, still half asleep, and slobbered a wet kiss on his bare feet. Joey rubbed him between his ears, just the way Buddy loved, and his whole body shivered and stretched as he wagged his tail in happy rhythm to Joey's massaging.

"Okay Bud, go lie down," Joey softly whispered. Buddy gratefully complied and after he settled himself back down in front of the radiator in the dining room, Joey eased open the door to the basement and fumbled around in the dark trying to find the light switch at the top of the stairs. Instead, his toe found one of Jerrold's toy trucks.

"Holy shit!," Joey yelped, as his foot reacted to the unexpected obstacle and slid down the first several steps, causing him to land hard on his butt. Reaching out his hand to grab the railing, Joey pulled himself to his feet and eased his way toward the bottom of the steps. Dazed by the shock of the fall and the searing pain from his ass, he was totally unprepared for the crescendo of torment that whipped across his head, threatening to split it open from ear to ear. Joey swooned and stretched out on the steps for a good while, struggling to stay conscious.

"Lord, this is going to kill me yet," Joey softly mumbled as he struggled to his feet, flipped the light switch near the bottom of the stairwell in the basement and limped down the last two steps to reach the floor. Once safely on solid ground again, Joey picked his way around assorted toys and piles of regular suburban junk to his office, the Sanctum Santorum as Carmen called it, locked the door from inside and reached behind his prized leather-bound edition of the Oxford English Dictionary, a gift from his late father, and entered a code on a hidden keypad. There was a soft rumble as the seals decompressed and the servo-drives whirred into action, opening the bookcase wall to reveal a secret chamber. Joey stepped inside and sank heavily into the lone seat in front of an impressive array of LED monitors as the wall slid back into place, sealing him inside. Joey flipped the switch nearest to him and the main monitor burst into life.

"Greetings and salutations!" Frank McBirney's chipper voice boomed from the screen, causing Joey to wince slightly from the sudden reverberations inside his still tender head.

"Hi, boss," Joey replied, trying to stifle a yawn as he felt suddenly overwhelmed by a sleepy weariness.

"You look like hell, Joe, what's up? Carmen demanding more than that big Nigerian dick can handle? I can slip her some of this hot Irish sausage if you need a break."

Joey smiled wanly at Frank's weak attempt at straight guy talk. Why do gay men always have to talk about sex? Joey wondered.

"Well, for one thing, you're buck ass naked, dude!" Frank barked, grinning from ear to ear like the cat that ate the canary. "And the last time you sauntered in in your birthday suit you couldn't keep from braggin' how blue your balls were after giving her the old in-'n'-out on the kitchen table while the kids were at your mom's house, okay?"

Geez, I must be tired, Joey thought to himself. How could I forget that Frank is an Empath? He tried to concentrate on keeping his thoughts below Frank's sensitivity level.

"Sorry, Frank, I'm just trying to deal with this massive headache."

"Hmm, a real ballbuster, huh?" Frank smiled wickedly. "Oops! Did I do it again?"

Frank was incorrigible. Still, Joey had to admit that Frank was a marvel of psychic ability. At 36, though looking at least a decade younger than that, Frank McBirney had scored off the charts on remote viewing skills and at least four academic papers were dedicated to his astounding telepathic acuity. He had made his professional reputation during the War on Terrorism, when he single-handedly intuited the exact whereabouts of one of the most wanted international terrorists, Sheik Mohammed Al Abedi, who had been well down the path with a plan to destroy the Eiffel Tower. Thanks to Frank's astral projection skills coupled with deep mind probes of prisoners at one of the CIA's secret rendition bases, the would-be suicide bombers were apprehended before they could carry out their plans, saving untold thousands of lives.

"Seriously, Frank, it's different this time. The pains are sharper and deeper than any I can recall. I think something really huge is brewing this time."

Frank was now the head of Counter Intelligence Operations for PsyOps, an agency so secretive that maybe only one person in the whole civilian government knew of it. Added at the last minute during a late night conference committee between the House and Senate when the big Intelligence Overhaul Bill was passed way back in 2004, following the recommendations of the 9/11 Commission, there was no direct mention of it ever again in any budget appropriation and its headquarters, staff and mission were all anonymous, part of the so-called Black Box military infrastructure. PsyOps was short for Psychic Operations, and it liked to think of itself as the last line of defense between mankind and Armageddon. Though the Defense Department had been secretly funding research into a number of psychic intelligence projects over the years, it wasn't until hard successes like those of Frank and a small select group of similarly skilled people that real momentum built for creating an official unit devoted to using psychic methodologies, from remote viewing, astral projection and past-life regression to tarot reading, telepathy and telekinesis and a host of other disciplines.

"Any ideas on a time frame?" Frank asked, leaning forward in his chair and jotting down notes.

In this new conflict, Frank relied on people like Joey, lovingly referred to as 'Sniffers', so-called because they sniffed through the billions of random thoughts in the ether looking for signatures and patterns that could point to activities by hostile forces, the evil hordes as it were, in their early stages, providing enough time for PsyOps to mobilize the white hats to neutralize the enemy. It was grueling work since it required many long hours of concentrated focus trying to pick out and sift through a tidal wave of psychic information looking for small traces of useful data. There weren't too many Sniffers who lasted more than six or eight months at most, but Joey was a natural, having worked for over six years and showed no signs of tiring or burning out. Joey was the Gold Standard of Sniffers. Frank had been getting a steady stream of reports from others, but it was Joey's report that he was waiting for. Joey was the best Sniffer in the service, he and Frank had served together on dozens of missions, and if he was feeling something out there, then It was definitely out there.

"Any sense of what or where it might be?" Frank followed up before Joey could answer.

Joey winced with pain and clutched the edge of his desk. He struggled to get his words out.

"Not really. The pains are coming every few minutes, so if anything, I'd say it's probably sooner rather than later. There seem to be a lot of points."

"Multiple attacks. Not good."

"Yeah, but also concentrated in a way. I'm feeling like there are a lot of forces targeting one central point."

"Are you sure, Joe?"

"Well, I'm as sure as a guy can be at 2:30 in the morning, buck ass naked, sitting in a freezing basement, with a massive headache like he's drunk half the liquor this side of the Mississippi and needs to piss something fierce!"

Frank chuckled. "Now, that will look really good in my report. Repeat that for me so I can quote you verbatim."

"Well, I'm glad you can find some humor in it."

"Ah come on, Joe, you know I'm just joshing with you. I realize how deadly important this is, believe me. I lost my twin brother during the Irian Jaya campaign, remember? But damn it, I have to find a way to not let this stuff overwhelm me and humor is my weapon of choice, okay?"

Joey flushed with embarrassment. Irian Jaya was nasty business and a lot of American troops lost their lives during the covert invasion of that miserable province of Indonesia that shared half of the island with Papau New Guinea. A militant insurgency had started high up in the verdant valleys that flanked the Maoke Mountains, which formed the dominant backbone of the island. The insurgents had been agitating for the overthrow of the Indonesian government for decades, but after the bombing of the Twin Towers, they became a more ominous threat as radical Islamic extremists groups around the world funneled money and weapons to their cause. Sometime around 2018, it was discovered that a group of nuclear scientists who had fled Libya before the fall of Muammar Gaddafi were working to build dirty bombs with technology they had spirited out of Tripoli, augmented of course by new materials and weapons-grade plutonium from Iran and North Korea. Not wanting the bombs to fall into the hands of terrorists, but wary of making yet another large scale incursion onto foreign soil in defiance of world public opinion, President Clinton (Hillary this time, not Bill,) sent clandestine teams of Navy Seals, supported by PsyOps astral projectors, into the lush jungles of the Sungai Tariku river valley, which drained the glaciers on the high peaks of the Sudirman Range that comprised the western portion of the Maoke Mountains, and was largely known to casual outsiders for its copper and gold mining operations if it was known at all.

Unbeknown to anyone, however, the insurgents on Irian Jaya were not your garden variety terrorists. They had hooked up with the worst of the Satanic Cargo Cults, complete with human sacrifices and reports of widespread cannibalism. After the Esh Shaubak Affair the previous year, when PsyOps attempted to assassinate Ahriman (aka Satan) near the Gate of ADAR, there had been a resurgence of wicked cults all over the globe. But none was as bad as that at Irian Jaya. Though the mission was ultimately successful in destroying the Libyans' bomb-making operations and breaking the insurgency, the cost had been horrific and most of the families of the fallen couldn't be told anything about what happened since officially the mission never took place. Frank knew because he was an Empath and was always in constant touch with his twin brother Sean. Joey knew because he had been one of the senior mission techs monitoring the astral projectors, who had mastered the ability of multiplying their psychic manifestations thus increasing the forces on the ground by the tens of thousands, something that would have been unthinkable if done with conventional troops. PsyOps was only just barely able to keep the lid on the torrent of fallout that followed, since the forces of Ahriman went into overdrive seeking revenge, and they were still out there causing trouble.

"Sorry, Frank, it's just, this pain. It's intense, man, really intense. I can barely hold it together here."

"I feel ya, Joe. No harm no foul. Why don't you get back to Carmen before she thinks you're out whooping it up with that light-skinned Bajan hottie from down the block."

Joey was shocked for a moment, but then recalled the brief flurry of illicit thoughts that had crossed his mind when he was out walking Buddy last week and happened to spy the attractive new neighbor in the too-short shorts and tight-fitting halter top watering her lawn who had just moved in. Damn, he mused to himself, making sure to keep his thought waves below Frank's empathetic threshold, that man is always snooping around in people's private memories.

"One day Frank you're going to go too far," Joey snapped out loud.

"Yeah, I know, but until then…" Frank looked down at his console with a worried expression, letting his thought trail off. "Got to go, Joe, stuff's starting to boil. Keep up the good work." The screen went dark as Frank signed off.

Joey sat at the desk for a long while trying to put his severe pain in check by sending Reiki to his throbbing temples. At last, he turned off the monitors and closed up shop, making certain that no trace was left behind of the hidden entrance to his secret redoubt. Joey went back upstairs, stopping in the kitchen to grab a glass of warm milk. He gazed out the windows while the milk heated up in the microwave, watching a group of deer forage near the small pond out past the kid's swing set under a huge full moon slowly disappearing behind a thick veil of clouds. His body began to relax as the deer serenely went on their silent way.

"Thank God we're out here in the country", Joey mused. "I'd hate to be a city dweller the next few days."

As he gingerly stepped into his bedroom again, Joey prayed that there was still time before whatever was coming to get Carmen and the kids to an even safer haven. Being two hours from New York City suddenly didn't seem nearly far enough away. They had taken a family vacation to Saba the summer before and that rugged mountain peak in the middle of the Caribbean Ocean was starting to look pretty damn good right about now. Joey made a mental note to call his travel agent later that morning. He slid beneath the sheets and snuggled up to Carmen, still sound asleep and completely unaware that he had ever left. Her body was so warm that he felt himself getting turned on by the contrast with his own chilly skin. Feeling his aroused member poking her from behind, she instinctively eased herself on to him, drawing him tighter to her as he entered her. His beloved Carmen, Joey thought, keeping her satisfied was more than a life's work and he was happy to be the one she had chosen to be with. After two kids she was still as rock hard and solid as the breathtaking beauty who had first captured his heart some ten years ago, when they were both graduate students at Howard who shared a passion for politics and track. She had been a school record holder in the 440 and 1000 meter relays, while he ran steeplechase and cross-country. Her long lean body was superb and had drawn his initial attention, but her rapier quick mind and facile debating skills sent him over the edge when they were on opposite sides of the issues in their Constitutional Law classes. Try as he might, he just never seemed to be able to gain the winning argument against her. They became fast friends and then inseparable lovers before tying the knot after graduation. Now here she was, still smokin' hot and always ready to kick it with him. Damn, I sure hope we'll still be waking up like this ten years from now, Joey thought as he gently rubbed Carmen's breasts while kissing the nape of her neck.

"Please dear God, whatever else may come, just let me be able to still do this," Joey prayed silently, settling into a sweet gentle sex vibe with his beloved wife.

At that moment, Joey was struck by a searing jolt of pain that reached all the way down into his dick, causing him to prematurely ejaculate. Fortunately Carmen was still sound asleep despite the deepening of her breaths as she too neared climax. Joey pulled out and hurried back down to the basement. He had clearly seen the outlines of the impending apocalypse, which was going to make the aftermath of the Esh Shaubak affair seem like a tempest in a very small teapot by comparison.

"Frank isn't going to like this," Joey thought as he frantically punched in the code to the secret chamber. "But at least that horn dog can console himself with one more look at this big Nigerian dick," he chuckled as he entered the chamber, slumped into his chair and fired up the monitor.

2 – ESH SHAUBAK

All around Aaron, the dark shapes of the multitudinous hordes of disciples pressed against him, carrying him forward to the sepulcher, where deep from within its dank interior issued forth the low murmuring of thousands of voices chanting out the ritual words which will open the crypt and signal the beginning of this secret conclave, complete with an address by His Demonic Majesty, Ahriman, the Devil Incarnate himself, about the impending conquest of the world of mankind and the defeat of the Elder Gods at long last. It had been a long time in coming but finally, Aaron sighed deeply despite himself, he would have his revenge for the death of his beloved Khydyra at the hands of Ornias, one of Ahriman's most trusted lieutenants. Her power was still deep within him, as was that of her spiritual twin, Osiriniki, a son of the Elder Gods who had been betrayed by his own uncle, the sacred Hierophant of the Lake of Fire, while trying to prevent a previous attempt at breaching the Gate Between the Worlds. Aaron himself became embroiled in the ancient conflict, when by an act of Fate, he was transformed from human being into a fearsome Soul Eater and specifically charged by the Holy Trinity itself to lead the Sons of Light against the Dark Forces of Ahriman.

As a Soul Eater, marked by the deep red plume that sprang from his crown chakra, Aaron was one of a special caste of spiritual beings, ranked in order of their unique powers and closeness to the throne of God by the color of the plumes they sported, who could travel between the worlds, collecting souls from both the living and the dead, and growing powerful in wisdom and experience with every soul they took. Khydyra and Osiriniki had chosen him, Aaron learned after much reflection, as the vessel for their souls because it had been ordained in the Great Plan of the Elder Gods that Aaron was to perform one especially fateful mission on which the whole of creation would depend. Unfortunately, the Great Plan hadn't predicted the outcome of that mission…which Aaron had long ago resigned himself to doing everything in his power to make as successful as possible…whatever that was, including even his own death, if need be.

Much preparation by the Ancient Ones had gone into making this night possible. Using an incorruptibly loyal and finely tuned network of psychics and true believers, the word was quietly put out to the most adept and powerful practitioners of the black arts to meet on the thirteenth hour, of the twelfth new moon, in the month of Adar, exactly thirteen kilometers northeast of Petra, along the axis to the oasis at Esh Shaubak in the Jordanian desert. It was here that the Seventh Gate, the Gate of ADAR, had been systematically pried open after many centuries of hard, dangerous labor by the Brotherhood of the Red Death, the most loyal earthly followers of the Ancient Ones, to create a small shaft of access between the realms of the dark forces on the other side of the Gate and this world. The Brotherhood are the polar opposite of the Jesuits, God's Marines, who promulgate and protect the One True Faith. Instead, the Brotherhood promulgates and protects the interests of Satan on earth and they are rewarded with exceptionally strong occult powers for their efforts. They are a well-organized presence usually in the background of all the worst events in human experience.

The Gate of ADAR, (so named because, according to legend, when Moses was called to Heaven on the seventh day of the twelfth month of the Hebrew calendar he passed through this Gate and placed his sacred seal upon it,) like all of the thirty-three gates that the Elder Gods placed in the membrane separating this worldly existence from the spiritual realms, is all but invisible to any but those blessed with the Third Eye. While their capacity for seeing through the material planes must be especially cultivated through arduous training, some particularly adept Masters of the black arts succeeded in locating the Gate which, along with its location in one of the most isolated places on earth, thus enabled the Brotherhood to work all these many centuries virtually undetected. Undetected, that is, until one of PsyOps most gifted psychics happened to catch flashes of an impending holocaust that seemed set to engulf the world unless the work of the Brotherhood could be foiled and the Gate resealed again. That insight set in motion the plot to assassinate Ahriman and create confusion in the ranks of his disciples.

"Hence," Aaron mused silently to himself, "my presence here amongst this sweltering crowd on a bracingly cold night in a land of many secret sorrows, being slowly buoyed along by the chanting throngs to a rendezvous with an uncertain fate."

The scene was certainly somewhat familiar, Aaron thought, having previously fought a similar battle at the Reisinger Peribolus which enclosed the Gate of ELUL, now located in an old cemetery surrounded by the densely inhabited New York City borough of the Bronx, where his beloved Khydyra, a Seraphim who had incarnated to help lead the Sons of Light in battle against the forces of Ahriman, had been tragically killed while trying to save his life. It was a loss that still haunted him, despite the fact that Soul Eaters aren't supposed to feel love or grief or sadness. In the blackness of the desert sky on this moon-less night, the Gate of ADAR is an imposing structure, glowing red like fire and emitting a searing heat which has caused the throngs of dark-robed men and women to sweat profusely, adding their collective funk to the already foul stench of sulfur and rotted flesh emanating from the cavernous sepulcher at the base of the Gate. From somewhere within that foreboding structure, there is a crypt that connects to the small opening in the Gate from which the Lord of Darkness will enter in response to the hushed incantations of his followers.

Aaron looked cautiously around him, deliberately avoiding any direct eye contact with anyone, as he searched for the source of a suddenly familiar scent which raised all manner of alarms in his body. At any instant his true identity might be discovered, thus placing him at risk of an undeniably hideous death. While there were certainly other Soul Eaters in amongst the crowd, each keeping a respectful distance from the others, Aaron was surrounded by the most practiced and capable seers, clairvoyants, magicians, sorcerers, necromancers, witches, warlocks and all manner of Adepts in the black arts and rituals of the Ancient Ones. With only the slightest gaze from their jaundiced eyes, his mission would be in jeopardy and the lives of many of his fellow comrades, who were waiting out there somewhere on the very far edge of the desert for his signal, placed in grave danger. He had spent many years training for this moment, trying to mask his thoughts and his powers so that he would not be detected by even the most suspicious of the Adepts. So it was quite the shock to feel the familiar signature of an enemy he had sworn to destroy at whatever cost emanating from up near the sepulcher. The Fallen Archangel Ornias, Ahriman's closest confidant and heir apparent, was here, Aaron concluded with a slight shudder. It was Ornias who had fired the terrifying blast of hellfire that had killed Khydyra and Aaron had been seeking to avenge her death ever since. Alone of the demon hoard which had poured into this world that day, Ornias had been trapped on our side of the Gate and thus incarnated in human flesh to sustain his spiritual essence in our plane. For the success of his mission, Aaron would have to set aside his desire to settle personal scores.

"I have to calm my thoughts," Aaron meditated, as he tried to compose his aura in order to pass through undetected by Ornias' intense scrutiny of everyone who came into the sepulcher for their devotion to the cause of his evil Lord.

He was now just a few dozen paces from where Ornias stood, still as magnificent and imposing as the first time Aaron had seen him, only this time the High Priest of Evil sported something new...the dark red plume of the most fearsome class of Soul Eaters, those like Aaron himself, who were the only beings other than God who could destroy another Soul Eater. Aaron smiled, at first involuntarily because it meant that now even he could take Ornias down, but then later because it seemed right to have the beatific smile of a true believer on his face as he walked right under Ornias' lingering glare. He had practiced cloaking his true thoughts around the aura of another so as to tag them with whatever indiscreet notions might inconveniently cross his mind. Just as a little test, Aaron laid a flurry of incriminating thoughts on an Adept about ten feet behind him. Ornias cut short his psychic investigation of Aaron and immediately focused on the hapless victim of Aaron's subterfuge. A corpulent elderly man was abruptly pulled out from the long line of congregants by several of Ornias' burly henchmen and taken quickly away to an almost certain death. The slight diversion allowed Aaron to work his way through the crowd in front of him to secure a very choice location from which to observe the proceedings. The chanting grew louder, ringing in his ears and echoing in the hollow of his chest, as slowly, almost imperceptibly, the crypt began to open, signaling the impending start of the coming rites.

It had been Frank McBirney's idea to carefully shadow the movements of several members of the close-knit circle of psychics and Adepts practiced in the black arts in preparation for this evening. The plan was to find relatively vulnerable practitioners who were susceptible to imprinting by remote telepathy but who would also not become aware that the imprinting had in fact been done. This was no small feat, since to become an Adept in the practice of the black arts all but insures that the practitioner will be very highly skilled and developed in the paranormal disciplines. After a couple of tragic false starts, which by themselves may have provided some warning of the impending action to come, by luck or good fortune three exceptional targets fell into PsyOps hands, two males and one female. Of the three, the most suitable for Aaron's purposes was a young, thirtyish Latino male, single, with a reed-thin build and a tendency toward hypochondria, since in the relatively cold mountainous climate of his native Bolivia he quite often came down with severe colds and fevers of mysterious origins and prolonged durations. Given the near constant self-medicated state he preferred, it was impossible for him to become aware of either Aaron's psychic presence or his brain patterns as

Aaron practiced laying them over the young man's own unique signature. In time, Aaron came to know the young man's every thought as if it were his own, which made the process of remote telepathic imprinting all the more successful. As it happened the young man was also very skilled in the practice of an ancient form of Voudou known as Candomble, a South American variant of West African voodoo but much more potent. PsyOps' big break came when the young man became one of the first cadres of Adepts called when the forces of darkness were ready to assemble.

Because once the operation got under way there would be no room for error, PsyOps decided fairly early on to go with all three of the selected targets and to have Aaron practice splitting his psychic energy amongst them simultaneously. He practiced throwing his power, much like a ventriloquist throws his voice, until he could obtain any result he wanted, at any time, from any or all of the targets without detection by PsyOps' very best and most sensitive mediums acting as a control group during the experiments. Aaron would sit right in front of the mediums and look them dead in the eye, while throwing a major bolt of psychic energy from one of the targets to a designated marker some fifty meters away from them, completely destroying the marker and leaving the target unaware of their role in the effort. From closed-circuit monitors and using human remote sensors, PsyOps had calibrated each test to achieve maximum destructive force with minimal psychic effort, so as to not leave any psychic signatures that could trace the force back to its point of origin. Being trapped in a chamber of clairvoyants, mediums and psychics with superior paranormal skills was no place to be caught sending out destructive bolts toward their supreme leader. The moment the bolt left its point of origin, the collective power of every one in that space would be directed toward the perpetrator with deadly results, thus the need to divert suspicion and create maximal confusion as to the exact source of the fatal bolt.

Though the crypt was packed to capacity with thousands of bodies chanting in unison in the near total darkness, Aaron now gingerly felt around the chamber for the signatures of his three unwitting assistants. The young Latino man, who would be the primary carrier of Aaron's psychic projections, was just a few meters away from him, to his left and down a bit due to the slope of the floor towards the front of the crypt. He was doped up pretty good, tonight, Aaron noted wryly, what with the pills for his bad head cold and the lingering effects of the dozens of prophylactic shots he was taking to stave off one of the many diseases common in this part of the world. He was not quite in Aaron's line of sight which was a very fortunate happenstance, in the event that the collective retribution that would be directed at him spilled over to those in his immediate vicinity.

The lone woman target, an Afro-Cubano who originally hailed from El Cobre in the Oriente Province, long known for its strong Santeria roots, but now made her home in South Florida and had a lucrative business performing black magic on behalf of spurned lovers, was certainly the strongest psychic of the three but prone to sudden epileptic blackouts when her powers peaked which made her somewhat unstable to control. She was clear across the chamber, on the other side of the crypt and just a step back from the edge of the stone platform, cordoned-off now, where presumably the Great Satan himself would soon stand. The other male of the group, the elder of the targets, was a descendant of a long line of Ashanti priests and an extremely gifted occultist. But he was also a rather brooding fellow given to fits of hysterical self-destructive tantrums which came upon him without warning, possibly due to the fact that the particular form of magic he practiced involved some really despicable, repulsive things, like the body parts of children and such, which should rightfully drive him insane. The Ghanaian was shifting quietly back and forth, from one foot to the other in a pantomime of a restless youth who badly needs to go to the bathroom, about fifty meters away from Aaron and some two meters back from being directly in front of the crypt, another potentially providential position Aaron noted. So here we are then, PsyOps' happy little family of doom, Aaron mused wryly, as the Great Archangel himself, Ahriman, finally rose up from the depths of the crypt to the now hushed assemblage of his adoring followers.

Truly, there is no sight grander than the Lord of Darkness in all His glory, for unlike what the fairy-tales may suggest, Satan is no monster but rather the most perfect and beautiful creature either in Heaven or on earth. It was easy to understand why God was so pained by Ahriman's treachery, since who could not have loved such a thing of sheer majesty as Satan? Though well advanced in years, he was still magnificent in his pulchritude. Standing some 7 meters tall, barely able to keep from striking his huge head, crowned with rams horns, against the top of the crypt, his face is like chiseled marble, with strongly defined features softened by unexpected and delicate nuances, like the full, ripe lips above a prominent square chin with a gingerly carved cleft; and the narrow, straight nose which flares just a hint around the nostrils, revealing the soft edge of fine down-like hair that clings to their edges. His indigo-blue eyes stare into the infinitude of space and time from beneath heavy brows, covered in unruly golden waves of hair streaked with flecks of snowy-white rivulets. His high forehead has no creases and smoothly flows into a still ample hairline, marcelled and coifed to such a fine sheen that his hair glows like the halo he so long ago lost. His torso is sleek, muscled and almost hairless save for a furry trickle which drips from the center of his chest, barely outlining his strong pectoral muscles, and runs in a luscious line over his flat stomach and into his bristly pubic hair. The flowing white wings curving from his shoulders down to his bare feet are powerful in their repose and twitch at the tips as if they yearn to stretch wide and lift off into flight, but the low ceiling and narrow confines of the crypt have necessitated their frenetic agitation. His thighs are huge, like the thighs of a well-toned runner's, and every tendon and muscle is cut and defined through the taut skin, which is covered in a thick matting of golden brown hair from his thighs to his ankles. Satan is naked and the grandeur of his tumescence has inspired the assembled throngs to cast off their robes and exult in the licentiousness that his eroticism inspires. Ahriman truly is God's most perfect creation and that he would have been God's heir had he but stayed in Heaven there can be no doubt, for the angelic entity standing before these hordes is the blessed incarnation of the Almighty Himself.

Aaron was about sixty meters away from where Satan stood, off to his right side, slightly outside the purview of his peripheral vision. His task now was to seek out any imperfections in Ahriman's magnificent body that might be evidence of potential weakness and to aim the explosive forces there, while not tipping off anyone in the crypt as to the purpose behind his intense scrutiny. The deep awe of the masses allowed Aaron to freely soak in every detail about Ahriman's body and to study each joint, each limb, each orifice, to note any flaw whatsoever. Satan basked in the adoration of His faithful masses, and seemed to draw strength from their admiring stares. As He preened and turned to give everyone a better view of His unimaginably beautiful physique, Aaron glimpsed ever so briefly with his intuitive senses the flaw he was looking for. The excitement of the discovery nearly caused him to shine like a candle in a dark room, but the intense training kicked in and he was able to keep his head (and senses) under control, as he probed ever so gently the small vulnerable spot just under and slightly behind Ahriman's right armpit, just beneath where his wing connected with his latissimus dorsi muscle. Aaron could sense that this small flaw was an old injury that had not healed. Was this a vestige of Satan's great fall from Heaven, Aaron wondered, and was this ancient wound the source of Ahriman's constant pain and torment, and hence ire toward the God who had cast him out? As fascinating as this speculation was, however, it was necessary for Aaron to set the plan into motion and complete his mission.

As Ahriman turned from side to side to accept the warm gratitude of the assembled masses, Aaron felt that it would be wise to take the shot as Ahriman turned His body away from the unwitting young Latino accomplice. Then, too, if Aaron hit Ahriman from where the Cuban woman stood, it might cause Him to veer even more sharply toward His left, thus exposing His vulnerable spot to both the young Latino man and the Ghanaian accomplice. Suddenly, Aaron felt a surge of energy slicing across his face in a desperate attempt to seek out the source of an unwanted intrusion. He knew instantly that it was Ahriman looking for him, having felt the very gentle probing Aaron had done of His wound. Aaron decided to strike at that instant and had the Cuban woman send an intense bolt of energy directly to Ahriman's left temple while the two men simultaneously directed their bolts at the soft spot of vulnerability near His armpit as Ahriman swirled from the impact of the first strike. The force unleashed as the bolts struck their mark was nothing short of spectacular, as a massive chunk of Ahriman's brain exploded across the crowed mass of followers near the front of the crypt, showering them with His blood and bits of bone fragments from His skull. The twin blasts to Ahriman's side succeeded in ripping a gapping hole into His chest cavity, smashing His rib cage, deflating a lung and damaging a significant part of His heart. Ahriman's body heaved upward and pitched wildly as the bolts hit and He staggered once then fell in a delicate pirouette over the edge of the crypt and into the mass of stunned followers at His feet.

The chamber erupted into a frenzy of panic, fear, and vengeful rage as the blood spattered onlookers sought out the three accomplices, whose bodies glowed fiercely from the power of the energy bolts emanating from their locations, thus stamping them unequivocally as the perpetrators of the most heinous act in Hell. The mad furry of the crowd was directed full force at the three assassins and their bodies, as well as those of a few dozen unlucky bystanders, were vaporized in a bloody mist of bone and shattered flesh which filled the suffocating confines of the sepulcher with an oily effluvium. Meanwhile, from out of the recesses of the crypt three of Ahriman's retainers rushed to His near lifeless body and tried to stop the bleeding from His wounds by stuffing them with improvised bandages made from the discarded robes of the faithful scattered about the floor. They quickly placed Ahriman's body into a makeshift stretcher and spirited Him back down into the crypt and presumably to the administrations of His attending healers. It was then that Ornias, momentarily stunned by the shocking events then unfolding, regained his composure and flew into a horrific rage, firing scathing shots of blue flames all around the chamber, setting everything and everyone ablaze as retribution for the ghastly assault. The chamber was filled with even more pandemonium as several thousands of Ahriman's followers suddenly found themselves on fire.

In the mass confusion of those storming the only exit from the crypt, Aaron quietly slipped away and made his way across the desert to a previously agreed upon meeting place to give his report to the first relay in a chain of messengers who would ultimately send word of what had happened back to PsyOps HQ. Aaron sincerely hoped that the damage done by the blasts was too extensive and massive to be reversed and that, once and for all, the Great Satan was dead. Certainly he was glad that he could at least take some small measure of satisfaction from the fact that he had done to Ornias what Ornias had done to him…taken from him the one being he truly loved and cared for in all creation. Little did he realize at that moment that what seemed like a near perfect mission was in fact only the opening salvo in the very Armageddon PsyOps had been trying to prevent.

3 – A TROUBLED DAWN

Frank McBirney shut off the monitor and stood up from his chair.

"Damn bastard!," he thought to himself as he replayed the image of Joey seared into his mind while rubbing the thick protuberance bulging at his crotch. "Why does that man insist on making his reports buck ass naked, especially after fucking his wife? He knows damn well I got a thing for black guys."

Frank paced in a tight circle next to his desk, in a semi-private corner of the cavernous multi-tiered control room that was at the heart of PsyOps Central Command, located in what had once been an old multiplex movie theater in a strip mall on the outskirts of Bethesda, Maryland, just off the Mainline to Chevy Chase. From the outside, the building still gave off an air of nondescript suburban blandness, which perfectly counterbalanced the deadly seriousness of its stock in trade.

"Shit, how am I supposed to go into the CO's office and give my report with this damn boner poking out of my pants? Goddamn fuckin' sexy beast!"

Frank smiled nervously as he looked around to see who else was still on duty at this time of the morning. Not many controllers worked the late shift since their operatives, unlike Joey, rarely felt the urge to report in, making for long, stultifyingly boring nights.

"It wouldn't be so bad if he was some kind of troll or something," Frank murmured under his breath, "but Joey's one fine dude!"

He spied only one other controller in the room, who was sprawled back in his chair and obviously sound asleep.

"And not a bad ass on him either. Hell, I'd do him in a heartbeat. Carmen sure is one lucky lady."

Frank absentmindedly shuffled some papers around on his desk, waiting for his bulging crotch to recede to a more respectable level. Going over the details again of Joey's last message helped to take his mind off of his more prurient thoughts.

"Damn, I'm sure glad I don't live in New York City anymore," Frank said with a long sigh. "I just don't know if we can stop everything that's headed their way."

He gathered up his tablet computer and checked the notes he had made as Joey gave him the latest relay. Satisfied, he felt his crotch one last time to make sure he was presentable and then walked up the aisle to the top tier of the control room. He placed his hand in the biometric scanner and waited for the vault-like door to slide into its wall niche so he could enter the security chamber.

Firmly placing his feet on the outlined positions marked on the floor, the door closed behind him, sealing him inside the vestibule. He stood perfectly still while the secondary and tertiary biometric scans were done on his body and psychic signature before the exit door finally opened onto the hallway that lead to PsyOps' main command wing. At the far end of an otherwise drab corridor was the surprisingly beautiful and ornately carved entrance to the suite of the Commanding Officer, which belied its former role as the main projection booth for the old movie theaters. The CO carried the military rank of a four-star officer and had a direct, though rarely used, channel to the Chairman of the Joint Chiefs of Staff, which had nominal oversight over the agency. But in practice, PsyOps didn't much use military protocols and reported regularly, and secretly, to only one person – the President of the United States. With what he was about to relay to the CO, Frank felt certain that somebody in the White House was about to get a very early wake up call. The last time he had to deliver news like this was when the Irian Jaya affair boiled over and that wound up costing several thousand innocent lives. It was a lot of blood for anyone's conscience to bear, particularly for those directly responsible for putting those lives in danger in the first place, thought Frank, and made even worse when close personal relations were involved. He shuddered involuntarily as he reached for the handle to the CO's office.

"Well, it's show time Frankie boy," he said out loud, as he smiled wryly and went inside, quickly patting himself down one last time just to be sure.

Graciella Montalban was at her desk, or more accurately she was hovering just above the big, oversized leather chair behind the impressively broad expanse of the clear mahogany desktop, in a deep state of trance that Frank had seen many times before. It was nonetheless still somewhat startling, especially for first timers, to see up close an illuminated Master Adept at the height of her powers in full synchronicity with the Akashic plane. As an Empath, Frank could intuit only the briefest glimpses of the worlds she was travelling through or the beings she was consulting with. But he also knew from first-hand experience that he could probe only just so far without being soundly and painfully rebuked for intruding on her psychic channel. Though Graciella might look to be in another state of consciousness, she was nonetheless fully aware of what was happening in her immediate surroundings as well. In fact, it wouldn't have surprised Frank in the least if Graciella already knew the substance of the report he was about to give. That was the way Graciella worked – she gave all of the controls plenty of room to manoeuver and arrive at conclusions which she had pretty much already foreseen. She used their reports as the ultimate confirmation for what her ethereal informers had imparted, mainly as a check on the incorruptibility of their information since after the Esh Shaubak business there had been a wholesale upheaval in the Akashic plane, with spiritual beings seemingly shifting sides between the Sons of Light and the Forces of Ahriman on a daily basis and biasing their information according to their current allegiances. Frank wearily sank down in one of the low-back club chairs facing Graciella's desk and waited for her to acknowledge him.

"Poor Frank," Graciella thought, as she zeroed in on his brain waves while still deep into her trance. "He's been given a vision of what is coming and it troubles him." She let out a long, deep sigh as her spirit began its return to her earthly body. "Now we will see just how committed Antipas is to our cause," she thought as she felt the weight of gravity slowly begin to pull her back down into her chair. "Our fate rests in the hands of a damned Soul Eater. May God have mercy on us all!"

With one final lunge through the barrier between the world of spirit and the world of flesh and bone, she was back, again, amongst the living. This time was the hardest yet, she felt, as she ruminated on the yearning that kept pulling her towards the cosmic realms for good, never to return. As a ninth-ground mahāsattva, Graciella could certainly have heeded the siren's call and indeed not come back to this often depressing and painful reality known as life. But wasn't it Kṣitigarbha, another ascended master, who said:

If I do not go to the hell to help the suffering beings there, who else will go? ... if the hells are not empty I will not become a Buddha. Only when all living beings have been saved, will I attain Bodhi.

And so, here she was, again, ready to reach into the teaming bowels of life to rescue her imperfect charges struggling to become yet more perfect in their own way. She sat perfectly still, relishing the last serene remnants of her ethereal journey, before her eyes opened with a slight flutter, squinting slightly into the harsh brightness of the fluorescent lights overhead. She stared at Frank a moment, taking in the fine lines of his boyishly handsome face. He reminded her of the altar boys of her youth in Zacatecas, whose angelic faces barely hinted at the great mayhem in which they loved to engage, particularly when it came to tugging on the long pigtails of a not so ordinary young girl who was rumored to possess certain strange powers. He was of sturdy stock, barrel-chested, thick but muscular, with an unruly mop of bright red hair that gave him the look of a circus clown. She smiled. Not many circus clowns can handle a .357 Magnum the way Frank could, though. Definitely the type of guy one would want covering their back in a skanky Manila bar fight against long odds, as Graciella could affirm from personal experience. She smiled brightly as the long ago memory was rekindled.

"So, Frankie boy, what have you got for me today?" Graciella asked with a mirthful gleam in her eyes.

"Well Chief," Frank started, playing along with her, "I was hoping you could tell me!"

They both laughed out loud, breaking the tenseness of the situation, before mutually sighing as they settled back down to the grim news that Frank soon imparted. Joey was getting impressions of a massive attack, with multiple vectors, on a global scale. It was as if the forces of Ahriman were planning to unleash Armageddon in one fell swoop. It was also clear that the logistics for the operation were highly distributed and cunningly fragmented to make each individual component appear to be just a random act of terror. But there was more than a strong hint that the coordination and activation of the attack was centrally planned and at the highest levels of the demonic hierarchy. If Ahriman had indeed been killed at Esh Shaubak like they all assumed, then what was being planned was an epic act of revenge aimed at taking all creation down with him in retaliation. The psychic forces being corralled to pull this off were unlike anything that PsyOps had encountered thus far. By comparison, Irian Jaya was just a pimple on an elephant's ass. The unsettling thing, though, was that the timing of the attack was unknown. It could be days, weeks or even mere hours away. And that was the mystery that now consumed Graciella's thoughts.

"Is Joey sure, Frank? Is he absolutely certain about this?" Graciella asked, her voice taught.

"Yeah, he called me up twice and the last time he was in a cold sweat," Frank replied calmly, looking down at his notes again.

"You sure it wasn't because he had just had sex with his wife?" Graciella remarked evenly.

Frank whipped his head up from the screen of his tablet with a startled look that must have given away everything that had happened before he stepped into her office, because she took one look at him and broke out laughing. After he recovered a bit, even Frank had to admit that it was just a little funny after all and he let himself chuckle a bit at his own expense too. He should have known that Graciella would have foreseen everything…Every…Thing!

"Okay then," Graciella said in a clipped, businesslike tone, which signaled that there would be no more fun and games for the duration of the crisis they were fast entering. "I want you to notify all the controls that effective immediately all leaves are cancelled and everybody is to report to their duty stations at once. And get word to Antipas Pergamos that I want to see him at 0800 hours and he is not to be late, understand? Make it absolutely clear to him, Frank, that I want his butt physically in my office and on time for once! No excuses!"

Frank wrote down Graciella's instructions as fast as she spoke them, but even he had to pause over that last one. "Ah, Chief," he started tentatively, before Graciella sharply cut him off.

"Case closed, Frank. I know how you feel about him and under the circumstances I can't say I blame you. You have every right to feel the way you do. But Irian Jaya is ancient history and regardless of whatever sins Antipas Pergamos may be guilty of in the past, right now he's the only initiated master on the planet with the skills we need to even have a snowball's chance in hell of surviving what's coming at us. Do I make myself clear, Frank?"

"Yes ma'am," Frank replied tersely, his face screwed into a look of total disgust.

"Good. Better get a move on. I'm off to see the Big Man on Campus."

Graciella's face was a mask of carved stone and Frank knew there was no use arguing with her. He nodded his head affirmatively as he rose to leave. He also knew that the President was not an early morning person so he didn't envy the task in front of Graciella. Her news was sure to cause more than a little turbulence to say the least.

"I just hope you're right about Pergamos, Chief."

"So do I Frank," Graciella replied with a heavy solemnity, as she watched him head toward the door. Just before he opened it another thought flashed through her mind.

"Frank," Graciella called his name with a great tenderness that stopped him in his tracks. They looked into each other's eyes for a long moment before she continued speaking. "I promise you, there will be time to settle old scores soon enough. But just not now, okay?"

Frank held her gaze a moment longer then silently shook his head affirmatively. Graciella smiled at him as he opened the door and walked out into the vestibule, closing it behind him. Frank felt himself shaking like a leaf, from his legs all up through to the top of his head. He didn't know if it was from anxiety over the impending calamity or from the deep antipathy he still felt after all these years against Antipas Pergamos, the half-human, half-demon Cambion spawn who had been with his brother's squadron in Irian Jaya. He could still see the outlines of Sean's anguished face as it became clear to him that his mission had been betrayed. Six men were part of Sean's team and in PsyOps' standard operating procedure, another team had also been sent in as backup, in addition to an independent observer whose role was simply to report on events as they happened. Antipas Pergamos had been the observer assigned to Sean's mission. He had previously been on the backup kill team that had shadowed Aaron's mission at Esh Shaubak and there was also considerable debate as to whether or not he had actually been in the crypt when the assassination of Ahriman had taken place. The designated observer reported that he hadn't seen Antipas, who was tasked with making a second strike if Aaron's didn't take out the target. Antipas later claimed that there had been too much confusion in the crypt after Aaron's strike to know whether Aaron had succeeded and even if he hadn't, there was just too much pandemonium for another strike to have been made successfully. It had raised some red flags at PsyOps HQ because Antipas was also a Soul Eater and they were always questionable when it came to where their loyalties truly rested. But because of Antipas' unique combination of occult skills and Cambion heritage, which was considered something of a plus since it gave him special insight into the demonic mind-sphere, he had nonetheless been assigned to the Irian Jaya mission, albeit in a much diminished role.

Sean McBirney's men had left their basecamp high up in the rugged alpine stretches of the Sudirman Range, along the Carstensz Summit Ridge, which at 4,884 meters is a striking geological oddity, sitting as it does in the tropics yet possessed of still very active glaciers that rival the Alps or the Himalayas. Their goal was to climb the Idenberg Top and descend into a narrow basin near the huge Freeport gold mine and eradicate a deeply embedded encampment of especially vicious shapeshifters known as Drudes. Drudes typically take the form of an ugly, old, withered woman, who is, at the same time, very heavy. This old woman creeps into homes at night through the smallest of cracks and openings. Once inside, the Drude sits on a sleeping person's chest and possesses them. This particular bunch was under the direct command of one of the Fallen Angels, Berith, a former prince of the Cherubim who had incarnated on this side of the Gate Between the Worlds and now used his great powers to tempt human beings into genocidal rampages. He used the Drudes to create homicidal converts to carry out his infernal pogroms. It was nasty business all around, given the inhospitable terrain and the treacherous psychic landscape the team had to negotiate without being discovered. It is no light task to go up against Cherubim, they were after all the first objects created in the universe and ridden by the God of Israel as upon the wings of the wind. According to the Midrash:

"When a man sleeps, the body tells to the neshamah (soul) what it has done during the day; the neshamah then reports it to the nefesh (spirit), the nefesh to the angel, the angel to the cherubim, and the cherubim to the seraphim, who then brings it before God."

Even ones fallen into defiance against the Throne of Heaven, as were Berith and his co-conspirators Ahriman, Lucifer, Beelzebub, Leviathan, and Ornias among some of the more prominent, Cherubim were imbued with the power of God and it was a mighty undertaking to even contemplate taking one down. But that was the mission and Sean's team made good progress, under generally favorable weather conditions, closing in on the coordinates of the demon encampment. They had established a secure defensive position that was undetected by the demons from which they could observe their patterns and strategically determine when to make their move. One night, though, some of the Drudes, disguised in the shape of a wisp of smoke carried on a cold breeze emanating from the demon camp, infiltrated the tents of Sean's team and took possession of two of them. Those men then went on a killing spree, hacking to death the rest of the team as they slept with machetes. Sean had been on sentry duty when the rampage started and by the time he got back to the camp, he was the only man left alive. Confronting him were his two former compatriots, now hell bent on murdering him. Still believing that his mission could be salvaged, Sean didn't use the gun in his holster for fear of alerting the nearby demons. Instead, he tried to take on both men with his own machete. But being possessed with the power of Berith, they were able to overpower Sean and in a cruel and sadistic fashion, they hacked off his limbs one at a time and watched him bleed to death.

Antipas Pergamos passively sat a safe distance away and observed all of this yet he could have intervened to help Sean, maybe even save the mission besides. Certainly as a Cambion, he could easily have overpowered the two possessed men on his own, let alone with the able assistance of Sean. It would not have been a breach of PsyOps protocol for him, at the very least, to have saved Sean's life by alerting the backup kill team, who at that moment were only several hundred meters away on another ridge. But instead, he had done nothing and as a result Sean McBirney died a horribly painful and needless death and Berith and the Drudes were able to take out the other PsyOps team before escaping to spread yet more infamy on our world. Frank could never forgive Antipas Pergamos for that. Never. Yet this was the man he now had to call at four o'clock in the morning to give him Graciella's edict. God knows where his phone call would find Antipas or even if he would deign to answer it. Frank was used to dealing with the notoriously fickle Soul Eater mentality, especially after working with Aaron for much of the last five years. But the difference between Aaron and Antipas couldn't have been starker: whereas Aaron was solidly on the side of the Sons of Light and could be counted on to go beyond the call of duty to save the lives of his comrades in arms; Antipas always, always, left one wondering just what his game was. For all Frank knew, it could have been Antipas who alerted the demons about the PsyOps teams' location, maybe as a way to get some fresh souls to eat. He certainly didn't put it past Antipas to be so ruthlessly self-centered. And that selfishness is what made Frank's skin crawl, even more than Antipas' lack of compassion, since when the chips were down the only sure thing that held a civilization together was one's willingness to sacrifice one's own life for the salvation of one's fellow man. Compassion was nice, but in the absence of self-sacrifice there would be nothing or no one left to be compassionate for. If Christ had not died on the cross for our sins, then what hope would there have been for us to find salvation on our own?

"No good will come of it," Frank spat out in disgust, as he picked up his headset. "Antipas Pergamos is no good and no amount of wishing otherwise is going to make it any damn different."

4 – ARRIVAL

"NEXT!" the immigration officer barked, looking at the long line waiting to clear customs at the Queen Alia International Airport in Amman, Jordan.

A rail-thin man, in his late 40s, somewhat stooped by the heft of a large backpack and a heavy satchel slung across his narrow chest, with the beginnings of a slight paunch, bone tired after the long flight, pushed the pith helmet back from his forehead, reached down and struggled to wheel his two bulky suitcases, almost too much for him to handle, up to the desk. With a heavy sigh, he pulled his passport and plane ticket from the side pocket of his well-seasoned satchel and pushed them across the counter, trying to muster his best smile at the stern countenance glaring at him.

"Salaam! Masa ii-khayr," the stranger blurted in stilted Arabic, trying to sound most pleasant and courteous.

The officer looked derisively at the small, dark blue passport with the gold embossed eagle lying on the counter. "Name and place of origin" the officer asked in equally stilted English, looking suspiciously at the nebbishy stranger.

"Antipas Pergamos. I'm from Massachusetts," the stranger replied, "That's in the United States," he added, trying to be helpful.

The officer looked at Antipas for a moment without saying anything, then slowly swept his hand at all of the baggage in Antipas' possession. "How long will you be staying in Jordan, Mr. Pergamos?" the officer inquired.

"Oh, perhaps ten, maybe twenty days, more or less," Antipas answered, taking off his pith helmet and mopping his brow with the back of his hand, trying to get used to the heat and humidity percolating into the building despite the mightily strain of its air conditioning.

"What's your occupation?" the officer asked, while ruffling through the pages of the well-worn passport, looking at the numerous stamps from previous journeys to many countries.

"I'm a professor. I teach the history of early Mesopotamian and Sumerian cultures," Antipas replied as cheerily as he could, trying to sound the perfect note of obsequiousness, "at Williams College."

"I've heard of Harvard, Yale, even Amherst, but not Williams College," the officer derisively snorted, seeking to impress on the stranger that he was familiar with American society and not some backward camel driver, as he surmised most Americans believed of people in this part of the world.

"Well you're not alone there, I'm afraid. Not many people in the U.S. have heard of it either," Antipas offered helpfully. "It's pretty small and pretty isolated and, well, pretty, too." Antipas smiled broadly, hoping that the officer might appreciate a little humor given the heat, the long lines and the repetitive nature of his job.

"Are you traveling for business or pleasure?" the officer asked, again peering suspiciously at the bulky suitcases, overstuffed backpack and bulging satchel at Antipas' feet.

"Oh, strictly for pleasure, officer."

Antipas had been through this routine many times. Crossing borders had become something of a specialty for him, considering that his unusual name, dusky caramel complexion and dark features made him the constant target of more than casual interest wherever he traveled. He was certain that whatever the criteria used, he was bound to be pulled aside, having tripped some vague alert based on the terrorist profile of the day. Antipas generally chalked it up to just the universal FWB syndrome, also known as Flying While Black. The immigration officer would ask him a few more perfunctory questions, then direct him to another officer who would escort him to a small side room where yet another official would ask still more questions while yet another picked through his luggage with close scrutiny. Occasionally, he would be asked to strip, usually not because of any banned articles found on his person, but because of prurient curiosity about the well-rumored propensities of the Black male. In those circumstances, Antipas found that a well-endowed sense of humor and a ready smile often sufficed to defuse most situations.

The luggage would solicit even more questions, stuffed to beyond its capacity with all manner of exotic survival gear, voluminous guidebooks to mount an expedition to every country in the Middle East, sufficient medical supplies for a small field hospital, and enough changes of clothing that would be suitable from a formal high tea with a government minister to serious horse-trading with merchants in the souk; entirely too much stuff for one wisp of a man so far from home ostensibly traveling for pleasure. His passport didn't help much either, particularly in those parts of the world where being an American was an invitation for trouble rather than being welcomed. But Antipas was ready and remained humble and at-ease, despite having been up for the last 28 hours, stuck in cramped airplanes, waiting for hours in noisy terminals, rushing to far-flung gates to make connecting flights and suffering the hideous gruel that passed for airline meals.

"That's quite a bit of luggage for a pleasure trip," the officer quipped, while tapping the open passport on the countertop.

"Well I hope to be going on an archeological expedition in the desert, near Petra. It's quite a hobby of mine," Antipas offered good-naturedly, knowing what would come next.

"I see. We have had quite a bit of our history looted by thieves from abroad. Black marketeers in ancient artifacts. Step over there," the officer sneered as he snapped shut the passport and motioned for one of the uniformed guards to come over at once.

"Here we go again,"Antipas thought as bent down and grabbed the handles of the enormous suitcases and began wheeling them toward the guard. He shuffled along in front of the unwieldy baggage, trying to maintain his balance between the backpack and the constantly shifting satchel strapped across his chest, beaming a broad friendly smile all the while.

After yet another two hours of perfunctory interrogation, during which Antipas repeatedly produced the letter of introduction from Dr. al-Noori, the head of the National Archeological Museum, who had personally invited him to join an expedition, and after several calls were made to various places, including one to Dr. al-Noori's office, he was finally released. Antipas pushed, pulled and dragged the heavy suitcases out of the airport terminal into the languid heat of the noonday sun, which seemed to suck the life out of everything not having the refuge of at least some shade, to hail a cab to take him to his hotel. It was a modest tourist-class place only slightly better than a hostel, in the

Jebel al-Ashrafiyyeh district on the slopes of the highest hill in the city, just south of downtown Amman. There, after a little more struggle, even with the help of an overly eager bellboy looking for a big tip one way or another, - "I can get you anything you want in Amman, just ask! Really, *any*thing!," - he succeeded in getting his luggage up to his room, where he was able to finally lie down and prepare himself for the work ahead.

No sooner had his head hit the pillow, however, there was a loud knock at his door. Half sliding off the bed, Antipas made his way to the door with great effort. When he opened it, he was greeted by a sweet faced girl of about fifteen or sixteen, swathed in heavy veils of a sheer fabric that left very little to the imagination. Antipas shook his head and vigorously waved his hands in the girl's face and shut the door without a word. He dragged himself back to the bed and fell face down on it. The heat was so oppressive that even in his supposedly air conditioned room, it crept into Antipas' bones and weighed them down as if his whole body was encased in wet concrete. He could barely move, even to remove his coat or take off his shoes. That's when the door shook even harder with even more insistent banging and didn't stop until Antipas again struggled to open it. This time, he found himself face to face with a very comely boy, again about fifteen or sixteen, with his tunic hiked up to reveal his ample endowment. And when Antipas rolled his head from side to side, the boy turned and bent over, offering up his firm, round buttocks. Refusing to be rebuffed, the boy tried to rub his naked bottom against Antipas' trousers, but Antipas managed to slam the door shut, smacking the boy's perky cheeks with the heavy wooden door, causing the boy to let out a loud yelp on the other side.

"Damn that bellboy," Antipas thought to himself as he checked the locks on the door again. '*I can get you anything*' "Well, what I *want* is to be left alone. Really!"

Slumping against the door, Antipas managed to kick off his shoes and slip out of his clothes before propelling himself headlong into the pillows on the bed, where he actually managed to sleep, if only fitfully, despite the cascade of thoughts raging in his head and the increasingly infrequent visitors announcing themselves in vain as the sweltering day slipped into sultry twilight. Of the myriad distractions, his thoughts were by far the bigger threat to any hope of a decent night's rest. He couldn't rid himself of the nagging, monotonous replay of his conversation with Graciella the morning before last at PsyOps HQ, itself announced with perfunctory efficiency by that little troll of hers...what was his name? oh, yes...Frank McBirney. Antipas made a mental note to himself: If fate allows, take that damned troll's soul! He had little use for the pugnacious Mr. McBirney.

Graciella, however, was an entirely different kettle of fish. Her message, delivered unctuously like the skilled politician she was – how else to explain her presence at the top of the heap at

PsyOps when there were so many more obviously skilled men available, not unlike himself, for instance? – clearly reflected three things: First, that PsyOps was out of its element given the threat swiftly careening its way; Second, they recognize that only Antipas Pergamos could possibly save them; and Lastly, they don't trust him worth a damn on account of his being a Soul Eater. At that last point, Antipas rolled over onto his back, with a slight chuckle despite being half asleep.

"These poor human beings," he mused silently, "they just don't get it."

And maybe, Antipas continued in a deep stream of consciousness, they might never really ever understand the complexity of the type of entities they are up against, even when some of those very entities are on their side, at great personal peril, he might have noted from his own direct experience. Then again, in fairness to these frail mortal creatures, how could they really be expected to understand the magnitude of the direct confrontation with consummate evil that the approaching apocalypse represented? The Four Horsemen were already riding their steeds, scythes at the ready, and the chains of Ahriman had indeed been loosed as the great Archangel Michael himself had predicted, low those many millennia ago. Only God's Warriors could possibly save mankind at this point…and Soul Eaters were the penultimate of the warrior classes of Heaven or Hell.

Soul Eaters are different from humans and just about every other type of spiritual being, angelic as well as demonic. They sit in the unique category of being totally agnostic about pretty much everything, on the whole. Concepts like good and evil are meaningless to them. They are like the ultimate cosmic truth detectors, relentlessly reducing everything down to its fundamentally essential objective fact of existence – something either is or is not. If it is, then it is either worth their paying attention to or it isn't. If it is worth paying attention to, then it is either something they should fear or something they should dominate. But since Soul Eaters only fear Yahweh, then everything else is a question of either domination or subjugation. So, really, from the perspective of a Soul Eater, creation is something that they must rule, since domination and subjugation are pretty much the same thing. Oh, and of course there is the matter of their rather specialized appetites, they are *Soul Eaters*, after all. And eating souls is a rather indelicate issue to human beings, since it is *their* souls that Soul Eaters have a taste for. So, Antipas concluded, looked at perfectly logically, Graciella and the rest of PsyOps are quite right not to trust him, since at any moment in time, any one of them could be his next meal, in a crude manner of speaking. And speaking of meals, well he *was* feeling a bit hungry, as a matter of fact, and the thought of snacking on that disagreeable troll Frank McBirney gave him a quite warm and fuzzy feeling that gently carried him off into a deep, blissful sleep at last.

When he awoke, it was dark. The clock by the bed said it was nearly three in the morning and the climate in the room at last felt slightly more hospitable. Antipas flopped onto his back and stared up at the ceiling, trying to decide if the rumbling in his stomach could be ignored until a more decent hour or if he would have to deal with it now. The violent churning seemed to realize that it would have to up the ante if it was to be heeded, so it threw waves of agitated acids at him, before finally succeeding in getting him to get up, if only to the bathroom. There, Antipas drank several glasses of water from the tap, knowing that he might regret it later but also calculating that it was time for him to begin acclimating to this place of exotic curiosities since there was no telling just how long he would be here. He searched through his satchel and backpack, looking for any scrap of something edible that might calm his angry guts for a while longer, since room service for what he needed was out of the question and he didn't think he wanted to prowl the streets of Amman at this hour to quench a transitory want that wasn't really life-threatening. All he could come up with were a few mints and half a granola bar of uncertain vintage. Holding the mints in one hand and the bar in the other, Antipas threw the mints down his throat and swigged another glass of water. He'd save the cereal bar for when he got much more desperate than he was now and stuffed it back into the satchel. Then he tried to sleep again until morning, but the mints only made his stomach more disagreeable than before.

"Okay, so it's going to be like that," Antipas sighed under his breath as he again rolled off the bed and began searching for his shoes in the semi-darkness. He rummaged about in the huge suitcases, feeling around for the right outfit that would render him mostly invisible on the streets of a hot, humid Arab country, hopefully even at this ghastly hour of the morning.

"There, this should do the trick," Antipas thought as he admired his reflection in the mirror. The long dark tunic looked just worn enough to suggest that its owner was only slightly better off than a common beggar and the thick keffiyeh hid his whole face except for a slit for his eyes, whose darkness under his heavy, thick eyebrows made him appear almost like a native. Pleased with the transformation, Antipas headed out of his room to search for something to satisfy his hunger. As expected, there was no one on duty at the front desk so Antipas checked himself once more in the mirror behind the counter and then headed out onto the streets. He paused for a brief moment in front of the hotel to reconnoiter the scene before letting his intuition and his stomach guide him in his search for food.

Antipas had specifically selected this neighborhood because it afforded a measure of obscurity for him, particularly when dressed in full Bedouin style, and his comings and goings would be less likely to catch unwanted attention. It was a populous working class enclave nestled close to downtown but just outside the more popular tourist areas. Nearby was the Wihdat, a low-income area of former refugee camps that still housed many Palestinians long after their escape from the then newly declared State of Israel in 1948, hard on the southern flanks of Jebel al-Ashrafiyyeh. He also liked that there were large numbers of transients just in from the countryside looking for work in the small shops of Amman, as well as plenty of the wily, citified miscreants who preyed on their naïve gullibility and exploited their vulnerabilities. The latter were of great interest to him, since they were certainly not going to be missed very much if they met with some unfortunate circumstance in the dead of night. Extracting a living soul from its human host was not a particularly pleasant undertaking, especially for the host, and it just made much more sense to fade into the general background of incipient criminality that already lurked in the shadows of the derelict precincts thereabout. As he stood on the steps of the hotel at that early hour of the morning, Antipas was pleased to find the street was mostly empty. To one side, across from the hotel, a surly-looking group of men were standing, engaged in some hushed but lively conversation judging by the pushing and shoving among them. They suddenly stopped and considered the stranger standing in the shadows near the front of the hotel.

"Must be the pimps," mused Antipas, thinking of the boy and girl from earlier who were probably servicing the hotel's more accommodating johns. Fortunately, after some long stares followed by a hurried discussion among them, the men quickly lost interest in him and went back to their jostling, deciding perhaps, thought Antipas, that he wasn't some unwelcome competitor trying to horn in on their turf.

"Probably think I'm just another common thief on the prowl," Antipas chuckled to himself. "And broadly speaking, they are more right than they know."

To the other side was a lone car with its driver fast asleep behind the wheel. Antipas recognized the man immediately.

"Well at least somebody is interested in my welfare."

He smiled as he hurried past the car where the immigration officer from the airport was soundly sleeping, taking a break, no doubt, before resuming his oh-so-discreet surveillance of the American professor from some obscure college no one ever heard of who was probably in Amman to steal more of the nation's ancient treasures. Up ahead was a small opening in a block of drab apartment buildings, leading to a narrow, dank alley that ran down a blind curve. Antipas smiled as he walked slowly down the alleyway, hugging the side of the buildings and blending into the many crevices and shadows that helped to hide his passage, almost giddy with the prospect of the chase for a ripe soul.

"Soon, mon ami, very soon," he murmured soothingly to his churning stomach. He sniffed the air as he walked, his nostrils flaring to gather in a scent that caught his attention. He smiled broadly.

"Ahhh, at last!"

Antipas bounded ahead, his footsteps falling silent on the cobblestones as he pursued his prey. The poor man would have no idea what hit him and in a split second, faster than one could blink, it would all be over without a sound. The rumbling in his stomach grew more insistent as the prospect of nourishment grew more certain.

"God, I do love it so," Antipas thought to himself as he sighted his intended target, stealthily casing the open window of a second-story apartment, and closed in for the kill.

5 – A FRESH START

The sun was high in the sky and, following a brisk morning of typical urban hustle, the sleepy little neighborhood surrounding the hotel was beginning to slink back into its usual mid-day stupor as the arid heat dug in for a long afternoon campaign that would only just slightly relent once its relentless master sank below the horizon. It took Antipas a few minutes to realize that the insistent thumping he only vaguely heard through the fog of his dreams was coming from the door to his room and not from his stomach, which would have been perfectly understandable given that members of his unique clan tend to be ravenously hungry practically all the time. He gingerly ventured opening his eyes and was greeted with a blinding flash of sunlight streaming through a small crack in the heavy shutters covering the room's only window. Reeling from the harshness of the light, Antipas pulled the wafer-thin, musty bedcovers, which if they had ever known better days were long past any memory of them, up over his head and waited for his sight to return to normal. The incessant pounding only grew louder and more urgent the longer he tried to avoid having to deal with the inevitable.

"Okay, whoever it is isn't going away," Antipas muttered sourly to himself, "so they're going to get more than they bargained for!"

He threw off the sheets and rolled out of bed, letting the momentum of the action carry him across the narrow width of the Spartan room to the door, which he yanked open with such force that the door handle came off in his hand.

"What!" he roared loudly at the top of his lungs trying to be as intimidating as possible, while standing stark naked in the doorway.

"My, my! If it isn't Antipas Pergamos. I see you still know how to impress a girl!" came the unexpected reply from an all too familiar voice, followed by a spasm of giggles.

Momentarily stunned, Antipas just stood there fully exposed, blocking the doorway, as Dr. Hanna al-Noori waited quietly for him to regain his bearings.

"Well? Are you going to invite me in or are you not alone in there?" Hanna giggled again as she tried to peer around Antipas into the room.

"Sorry, I wasn't expecting it to be you," Antipas offered meekly as he turned suddenly and searched for something to cover up with. "You look great, Hanna, really great," he called over his shoulder, slipping the tunic over his head.

At forty-five, dressed in stiffly starched desert fatigues that accented her curvaceous figure, Hanna al-Noori, PhD, still possessed the stunning model-perfect looks that had caused such a sensation when she was much younger, winning the Miss World crown in a unanimous decision and going on to dazzle the runways of Paris and New York while earning two doctorates, in economics and archeology, and publishing numerous very well-received articles and monographs in peer-reviewed scholarly journals. No one could believe that such a beautiful woman actually liked spending the better part of the year knee deep in hot sand digging for evidence of ancient trading economies in the middle of inhospitable deserts. But Hanna was both brilliantly passionate and ambitiously driven and scored coups that earned her both the respect and envy of her peers around the world. She made it look so easy, and then the way she looked just added more insult to injury.

Antipas had first encountered her at a United Nations-sponsored conference on World Heritage Sites some years ago, when they were seated next to each other on a plenary session panel. They had hit it off immediately, even though they had taken opposing sides on the issue before the panel and had argued vehemently over their differences. The passion of their argument seemed to have ignited a fire of a different sort between them and they were soon inseparable for the remainder of the conference, making a most unlikely pairing, her Beauty to his Beast. He liked the way her mind worked and she was drawn to the underlying strength and resolve that few people suspected he possessed. He was self-deprecating to the extreme, almost as if it were an act, she had once taunted, which he deftly used to control people and situations without their knowing they were being manipulated into doing exactly what he wanted them to do. He was so shocked at having been found out that she pushed him down in triumph and planted her foot in the middle of his chest, like a hunter standing over her trophy. All he could think about was how cute her pink silk panties looked from below and when she realized what he was doing, she let out a big laugh, pulled her panties down and squatted, rubbing her creamy, soft, café au lait-colored cheeks into his face while holding her balance by grabbing a clump of his hair by the roots and telling him 'Mistress was going to punish him for that.'

And she did, which was the first time Antipas had ever been dominated by a woman in that way and he found himself enjoying the sensation of it all more than he could ever have imagined. When she was finally ready to take his monstrous endowment into her, she had whipped, slapped and carved her claim into every one of his thick, ebony inches, making it feel as though his private parts no longer belonged to him and were only there for her pleasure and she would decide if they remained in his keeping for her use. He had never ejaculated as hard or as often when she at last allowed him to relieve himself after she had had her fill and was sated from riding him almost raw. Afterwards, she was so gentle in the extreme as she bathed his sore and bruised body and rubbed soothing ointments on the red welts her paddles and floggers had raised. When the conference was over, she jetted off to high-profile archeological excavations and made even greater new discoveries, eventually becoming the first woman to head Jordan's National Archeological Museum. They had talked only occasionally since that encounter and rarely saw each other except for one or two conferences in the ensuing years, where the ardor of that first meeting was deliriously reprised. Now, here she was in his room and Antipas was overcome with a mix of emotions and more than a little curious about what was surely to come next.

"I see someone hasn't forgotten who I am," Hanna teased, as Antipas' tunic formed a large tent over his crotch.

"He always did have better manners than me," Antipas joked as he looked at the hardening bulge eagerly straining against the light fabric of his tunic. He looked up at Hanna's face and then with a great flourish he knelt down in total submission to his Mistress.

"Now, that's the slave I remember. Mistress is very pleased, boy, very pleased indeed." Hanna walked slowly over to him and extended her booted foot just in front of Antipas' face. He reached out and cradled the gift in his hands while showering it with kisses.

"Yes, that's right," Hanna murmured in a low voice, "We don't have much time, so strip and lie on your back."

Antipas stopped his kissing, pulled off the tunic, spread it on the floor in front of Hanna, and then lay on it as she had commanded, his thick manhood pointing straight up and throbbing in anticipation of the sweet torture to come. Hanna took off the belt from around her waist and wrapped it around her hand, leaving just a short stub, with which she began to tease and slap the swollen protuberance waiting to receive her.

"I see you learned your lessons very well," Hanna exclaimed as she increased the intensity of her flogging.

Antipas absorbed her devious torture in silence, letting his mind concentrate on the sound of the belt striking his flesh, the sharp sting caused by its hard leather edges, the way the sensations of pain flashed through his system like an electrical current, buzzing into his brain and spreading in a warm glow all over his body, until he felt as though he was vibrating from head to toe at the same frequency as the electromagnetic pulses shooting from his deep purple member to his skull. Then, just when he felt as though he couldn't take any more, Mistress stopped and blew on his swollen gland, her breath cooling his raw swollen skin and heightening the sensations flowing through his body. Hanna, her back to him, lowered herself onto his well-flagellated member and rode it until she was in a frenzied trance. She consumed him. Her strokes were powerful and long, deep and short, clockwise and counterclockwise, until Antipas was writhing under her, powerless to escape from her scintillating caress, desperately trying to keep from exploding inside her as she rode him faster. He gazed at the creamy smooth skin of her back, the delicate trickle of downy black hair matted from the sweat of her exertions making a striking contrast with her swarthy complexion. He watched the muscles of her skinny thighs and taut butt stretch and contract as she rode him, rising up just enough so he could see his slick, coal-black shaft impaling her as her strokes grew longer. He felt himself getting harder as she gorged herself with insatiable abandon. Hanna swooned from the force of her own orgasm and he was able to twist her around to face him, as she fell into Antipas' arms, where they held each other tightly, neither one wanting to let go of the other.

"I'm both glad and saddened that they sent you, Tip," Hanna said gently, as she squeezed Antipas about the ribs and buried her face into his furry chest. "I'm glad because I get to see you again. But I'm sad because…" her words trailed off into silence, and she hugged him even tighter.

Antipas knew what she was trying to say and he reached up and brushed the hair from her eyes as he stared into her beautiful sweet face for a long moment before kissing her thick full lips deeply and with a passion that surprised him for its depth of feeling.

"If only there was more time," Antipas thought to himself, "just a little more time."

TIME.

The one commodity taken most for granted and which is ultimately the only one that most people would love to have more of. At whatever cost. For immortals, like Antipas, time would seem not to be of much concern, but even their world was subject to the constantly shifting sands of the hour glass. According to the Great Plan, written by the Creator at the very inception of His singular achievement, a new day was soon dawning and no amount of interference by His most powerful and intelligent creations – human as well as spiritual beings – could forestall the inevitable Apocalypse that was on the horizon. Not unless of course, by some miracle perhaps, there was another plan at work, deep in the background somewhere of which no one was even remotely aware, that would somehow save the day…or at least save some part of the known worlds, above and below. But Antipas didn't believe in miracles, let alone some Deux ex Machinas that would step in at the twilight hour with salvation for the righteous and deliver them to the Elysian Fields forever and ever, amen.

The mission that PsyOps was embarked upon, which he was entrusted with albeit with deep reservations on both sides, and of which Hanna was an integral part, was nothing short of desperation in the face of suicidal odds. In Antipas' mind, there was really almost no point in even making the effort. So why was he here? What was he hoping to prove? And to whom? As he held Hanna tightly in his arms, smelling the faint but heavenly aroma of coconut, almond and cardamom in her hair, feeling the rhythmic rise and fall of her body against his chest, Antipas stared into the dark void at the center of his soul and faced the silent demon which resided there.

"YOU!" he shouted within his inner self, staring at the hulking shadow of his nemesis. "I'm talking to *You*, dammit, LOOK AT ME!"

But the demon steadfastly refused to acknowledge his presence and sat quietly, absorbed within its own psychic machinations…waiting, perhaps, for a moment in which to exploit a perceived weakness on his part for some gain at his expense. It was a familiar game and they both knew the rules, of which the very first was – there were no rules. Cat and Mouse, with the roles constantly shifting, the outcomes always in doubt, the victor becoming the victim only to triumph once more, in an endless cycle that had been going on since the moment after he was first conceived. Human and Demon in a dance together from which they cannot ever be separated.

Cambion.

Half-breed.

Monster.

He had experienced both the torment and the ecstasy of being something other, different, singular, in a small world of beings whose very existence was beyond comprehension to the vast majority of human beings; and was of not a little controversy among the beings of the spiritual realms. A Soul Eater whose particular taste is for others of his own kind and the higher orders of angelic and demonic beings. A distasteful creature to be kept at a discrete distance and under constant surveillance least he revert to type and engage in his most unsavory sport.

Cannibal.

Antipas recoiled ever so slightly, and as he did so, Hanna shifted her head to rest it squarely in the middle of his chest, as if listening to the beating of his heart. He lay as still as he could, trying to control his breath and slow his heart rate so that its cadence lulled her into a deep restfulness – only restfulness and just barely, because Hanna could never really ever truly be said to sleep, being an incredibly capable esoteric Adept in her own right. As it was, Antipas wondered just how much of his mind Hanna was reading as she lay there looking, well, angelic. He sighed inwardly as his mind recalled the exact details of the many souls that he had taken over the course of many eons. Who would ever want to be the very thing he was? What horror! Even now, as he lay with the one woman who could even begin to understand him, he felt the deep, wretched hunger rising up in his guts like lava.

Even she wasn't "safe" from his ravenous cravings. At that thought, the beast in him finally stirred itself.

"So, Antipas," the demon sang to him in a high sweet voice dripping with sarcasm. "Have you finally come to your senses then? Without ME you are nothing! Only I can give you the very thing you most want and so desperately need…"

He started to respond to the demon but before he could do so, Hanna's voice was reverberating inside his troubled mind.

"There is still hope, Antipas. Though God's plan may be hidden from us, it is never without hope for a better outcome. Have faith, my precious, have faith. Do not listen to the voice of darkness which only knows its own unspeakable pain. I will show you the light and the way."

Antipas looked at Hanna's head resting on his chest. He smiled wistfully. Just then, Hanna raised her head and stared into his eyes, touching his very soul with her unshakable confidence in the eventual triumph of the Sons of Light against the forces of Ahriman. He held her gaze and then gently kissed her Third Eye.

"Okay, there's much work to be done!" Hanna abruptly announced as she rose quickly and rearranged her clothes. She brushed the stray strands of her hair back into place with her hands and then looked down at him, still lying on the floor at her feet.

"Get up soldier!" she commanded, as Antipas gazed in rapt admiration at her sublime self-assuredness.

"Okay," he sighed, rising to his feet and picking up the tunic. "but I have to tell you that I remain to be convinced about the efficaciousness of all this foll-do-roll."

"I'm afraid you'll just have to trust me on that." Hanna replied curtly, retrieving her cellphone from the pocket of her dungarees and flicking through some screens until she found what she was looking for.

"Here," she said, handing the phone to Antipas. "This is where we're going. It's rough country and even tougher to reach from here. Better get dressed. They're expecting us this afternoon."

"They? Who 'they'"

"'They' are a riddle, wrapped in a mystery, inside an enigma," Hanne replied breezily, her face glowing. "And *They* are just dying to meet you!"

"Oh joy!" Antipas muttered as he started to pick out some clothes to wear.

"You might want to take a shower now, since I'm afraid it might be the last one you'll be able to count on. Chop! Chop!"

Hanna made herself busy as Antipas headed for the bathroom. He had a very strong premonition about the impending meeting. While still not convinced about the potential for success, he begrudgingly had to admit that at least there might be a sliver of possibility after all. Hanna was not one to dwell on the impossible and if she believed that there was a way, then maybe, perhaps, there was. If nothing else, he reasoned, the journey ahead would be an amusing diversion from his morose inclinations. He stepped into the shower and reveled in the hot trickle of steaming water dripping from the heavily corroded spigot above his head. As the water washed over him, Antipas felt his mood brightening slightly.

"Well, old chap," he murmured aloud, "If this is going to be your last, you jolly well better make the most of it."

6 – ROCKS AND HARD PLACES

As the two of them roared through the mercurial chaos of midday traffic in Amman, Antipas looked at Hanna's profile as she expertly shifted gears and maniacally maneuvered the hulking behemoth of an ancient Toyota Land Cruiser like a sleek Formula One racer at Le Mans. Following her constantly roving line of sight, Antipas watched the mad jumble of modern housing blocks, run down shanties, stately mansions rising behind impressive gates and staid government buildings, shimmering in the brilliant whitewashed haze of an unrelenting sun sizzling just past its zenith and leaving the streets eerily devoid of any signs of life, rush by as they caromed up and down the many steep hills and through the sharp valleys and deep ravines which comprised the heart of Amman. In some respects, Amman is not unlike San Francisco, both being cities built on a series of hills overrun with houses, shops, markets, restaurants and businesses of every stripe and sprawling outward in ever growing rings of development that enrich prosperous businessmen and leave the unfortunate many behind in their wakes, though Amman lacks both the waterfront location and the quaint Victorian charm that make people lose their hearts in San Francisco. Amman is a city that is relatively modern in a subaltern sort of way and in a constant state of invention, since most of it was built after its ubiquitous British colonizers left in the 1940s. There are a few interesting ruins from its Roman-era past, but for the most part it is highly unlikely that Amman will be immortalized in song or tagged with some romantic nickname. No, if you lose your heart in Amman it's because the car you're riding in, like every other car around you, has just driven at an insanely high rate of speed into a crowded traffic circle without signaling and is attempting a maneuver that rockets you from one side of the cabin to the other all the while blowing its horn to warn contending drivers to get out of the way, since stopping or slowing down are totally beyond comprehension to your driver, as certainly seemed the case with Hanna.

"A penny for your thoughts," Antipas jokingly asked, as Hanna momentarily released her white-knuckle grip on the steering wheel to hastily brush an unruly strand of jet-black hair from her heavily-lidded eyes as she stared intently into the distance like a sleek lioness whose attention has just been roused by some sudden movement in the bush, her face gently glowing in the reflected light streaming from the windows. Hanna sighed heavily and absent-mindedly wound the strand around her fingers as she continued to gaze straight ahead. Antipas softly patted her knee.

"Hello, anybody home?" At that, Hanna turned slightly toward Antipas and just looked into his eyes for a moment, then took her free hand and quickly stroked the side of his face, before returning her gaze at the seething snarl of traffic in front of her. He tried to gently probe her mind, but her psychic barriers were in full defensive mode so he broke off any further attempts to discover the source of her obvious melancholy. They rode the rest of the way in silence.

After several near collisions and one last long dash for broke through a thick gauntlet of heavy traffic, Hanna brought the big Land Cruiser, gears grinding, brakes wailing like a chorus of castrati, screeching to a stop in a cloud of burnt rubber, smoke and gravel in front of the steps to the Jordanian National Archeological Museum. Hanna quickly pushed open her door and scrambled out of the driver's seat, leaving Antipas fumbling frantically with the latch of the passenger door and then hurrying up the steps after her to keep from being left behind, as she darted past the carved giant marble hand of Hercules in front of the entrance to the museum and disappeared inside the dark nondescript opening with its promise of relief from the searing sun. Antipas briefly paused at the great fragment of what must have been a huge exquisite statute of the god which stood in the inner sanctum of the Temple of Hercules, whose majestic ruins still commanded the heights of the hill nearest to the museum, and speculated about the mythical races of giants that seem to figure so prominently in the oral traditions of many cultures around the world. He felt certain that there had to be something to the myths, given the almost universal nature of them and smiled as he recalled the story his cousin had told him when they were both around twelve or thirteen, away at summer camp in the Adirondacks for the first time and engaged in the universal pastime of boys – comparing their stuff. His cousin had said that the giants were the offspring of some angels who came down from Heaven and made it with human women and God was so mad he threw those angels out of Heaven and then destroyed the earth in the Great Flood. Only, some of those giants had survived and their lasting genetic legacy was still evident.

"Big hands, big feet, big…" he chuckled to himself as he remembered his cousin imparting that bit of prurient folklore late at night, after the counselors had gone to sleep, to a rapt audience of pubescent boys shining flashlights down their pajamas to see how much giant blood they had. It was the one time in his life that he had won the enduring admiration of his peers and for the rest of that summer earned a fortune in candy and other favors for a glimpse of his unique claim to fame.

He hurried his pace when he realized he'd lost all sight of Hanna. It took Antipas a few minutes to gain his bearings once inside the foyer of the museum, since the contrast between the hot, glaring exterior and the cool, dimly lit interior had left him momentarily blinded, especially after his eyeglasses had fogged up with the sudden change in temperatures. He wiped them gingerly with his thumbs while trying to find any trace of where Hanna had run off to. He looked to see if there were someone who could help him, but the cavernous foyer was totally empty. He tried to stand as quietly as possible in hopes of hearing any noise or footsteps that might at least indicate the prospect of locating where she had gone. But that too proved futile. So he relaxed his mind and let his intuition guide him as he wandered aimlessly about the various corridors that opened before him, taking passing note of the superb collection of historical artifacts on display, almost assuredly found during one of Hanna's many expeditions into the surrounding desert. After a while, Antipas came to a long hallway with numerous doors opening off it, where he felt certain he could detect a faint whiff of Hanna's psychic signature still lingering in the calm air. He turned down the hallway, and stopped in front of each door, sniffing like a bloodhound searching for the scent of a missing person.

He was halfway down the hallway when suddenly a door at the far end slammed shut. Curious, Antipas hurried toward the sound and as he got closer, he heard loud, agitated voices and hands pounding on tables. They were mostly male voices, but he could make out at least one female speaker, though it wasn't Hanna. He was about to knock on the door to announce himself when a door behind him, across the hall, opened and Hanna's welcome voice called to him.

"Tip! What took you so long?"

He turned and saw Hanna's elegant figure silhouetted against a brightly lit room, where a handsome man in his early 50s, of swarthy complexion, average height, with a trim and compact build, dressed in a military uniform of a somewhat vague nationality, stood in the background.

"Sorry, I got hung up trying to figure out the lock on the car door and by the time I finally did, you had disappeared on me," he replied, with a mixture of relief and apprehension in his voice.

"Oh, my bad," Hanna smiled coyly. "I should have warned you it was broken. There's a trick to it." Her eyes glittered as she looked at the befuddled expression on Antipas' face, the very epitome of the absent-minded professor. She gave him a wink and gently patted his arm.

"Here, I'd like to introduce you to someone," Hanna said turning and briskly walking away, again leaving Antipas stumbling to keep up with her.

He entered into the room, a surprisingly large, even cheery, book-lined study with a huge floor-to-ceiling window offering a surprising view of a lush garden hidden in an interior courtyard, shaded just enough from the sun to look inviting despite the strong heat that nonetheless crept through the glass from outside. The stranger stood in front of the window, clutching a large, intricately embossed folio in one hand, while extending an exquisitely gloved hand toward Antipas.

"Antipas Pergamos, I presume?" the stranger asked in an accented English that was difficult for Antipas to place right away but which was certainly not Jordanian, his lips broadening into an engaging smile that had Antipas responding in kind despite his wariness.

"Indeed, and you would be…"

"This is Major Fraser," Hanna interjected, before the stranger could reply, "He's come a very long way just to meet you."

"Well, I'm flattered," Antipas replied dryly, "Does the Major have a first name?" he asked, looking directly at the man, who possessed an impressive golden plume above his head, marking him as being of a very high spiritual caste.

"Francis. Francis Racoczi Fraser, to be exact, but my friends just call me Rocky, which I hope you will too," the Major replied, keenly observing the dark, deep red plume above Antipas' head while smiling graciously.

"Pleased to meet you Rocky," Antipas said, trying to politely disengage from the Major's enthusiastic handshake. A very firm grip, Antipas thought to himself. Rocky was definitely not a man to be underestimated. "Racoczi, now where do I recognize that name from?" he said aloud, addressing the Major.

"It's Romanian, my family hails from Transylvania originally. We moved to Austria when I was still quite young and then later my father sent me to Italy to live with my Uncle Cosimo in Florence. The climate there was better for my health. I spent many pleasant years in San Germano, a small village near my uncle's estates."

"Shall we sit for a moment," Hanna suggested, motioning toward a comfortable circle of leather chairs arranged around a low table. Rocky bowed politely toward Hanna and waved his arm in an extravagant gesture for her to lead the way.

They made some polite conversation, about such innocuous subjects as the weather, the latest cricket scores, and the always tense situation of the Palestinian refugees, when Hanna signaled the Major to begin the substantive portion of their meeting. Rocky looked intently at Antipas, though in fact his eyes had never wavered from him since Antipas first entered the room. Antipas immediately noted how the Major's psychic attention bored into him. It was as though he could feel the man's mind penetrating his body, examining every cell and weighing his soul. It was an awkward feeling that Antipas felt left him intimately exposed, as if he were stripped naked in public and given a deep cavity search in full view of passersby. Antipas emptied his mind so as not to betray his innermost thoughts and returned the major's gaze, probing him with equal intensity. Rocky smiled at him and began nodding his head.

"What is it?" Antipas asked coolly, his face a total blank.

Rocky leaned forward in his chair, which was only a few inches from Antipas, took off his gloves, folded them neatly and laid them on the table, then reached out and placed a hand on Antipas' knee. He looked deeply into Antipas' eyes and the smile finally left his face as he spoke with a grave urgency that was both unexpected and tender.

"My friend, even though we have only just met, I feel like I have known you for an eternity of ages." The major then retrieved the folio from beside his chair and opened it, rustling through papers as he continued solemnly.

"Your dossier is just astonishing, your accomplishments are beyond comparison and quite reflective of your fine heritage. This mission demands only the very best that mankind can proffer and what better warrior than an august descendent of Ham! I salute you, Dr. Pergamos, I am just in awe of you."

Antipas felt the blood rushing to his ears. What kind of patronizing bullshit was this? he thought. He had put up with this kind of talk all his life, especially in the academy, where such pleasantries are used to obscure the bitter professional rivalries, doctrinal disagreements and internecine warfare over coveted fellowships, grants and that holy grail of all academics, the tenured position. Whenever he heard such praise, Antipas instinctively started sniffing the air for a hint of a more earthy scent. And what's with the reference to 'descendent of Ham'? Nobody dredges that shit up any more, except Mormons and Klansmen, and when they do it's because of the Curse. People are more familiar with the Curse of Ham than with the accomplishments of his sons. In fact, that Curse has been used to justify apartheid, excuse slavery, tolerate segregation and support the notion that Black people are somehow less than fully human.

But the Children of Ham can also be considered the people chosen by God to open up His creation after the Flood and make it habitable for the races of mankind. They went before, they plowed the earth, they blazed the paths for others to follow, they built the first cities and established the first civilizations and when they were scattered to all parts of the earth after the fall of the Tower of Babel, they settled its wild places and brought forth the full bounty of creation. It was Cush, after all, whose lands were surrounded by the second river of Paradise, and who fathered Nimrod, the mighty hunter, who founded the fabled Babylon. It was Mizraim who fathered the nations of Egypt and the civilization that would grip the imagination of mankind with the splendor of its monuments and the depth of its beliefs. And it was Phut who fathered the tribes of North Africa. Together, these sons of Ham gave rise to the Fertile Crescent that would yield civilizations whose mysteries and learning still captivate the world, countless eons since they first shimmered under Heaven's gaze. Ur, Chaldea, Assyria, Accad, Lydia, Ninevah were all built by the descendants of Ham. The first language, Akkadian; the first writing, cuneiform; the first library, King Assur-bani-pal's; the first codification of the law, Hammurabi's; the first epic poem, Gilgamesh; these are the legacies of the black-skinned children of Ham, these are the gifts they gave to the generations of mankind and these are the treasures that no one speaks of or remembers but which they still share with those who seek truth. And then there was Canaan.

"Cursed be Canaan; a slave of slaves shall he be to his brothers. Blessed by the Lord my God be Shem; and let Canaan be his slave. God enlarge Japheth, and let him dwell in the tents of Shem; and let Canaan be his slave."

That's all it took for the legacy of Ham to be forever under a dark cloud, made darker by the mindless willingness of men to think ill of one another as it suits their own purposes. A drunken father's curse not of his own son, but of his grandson, since to curse the son would reflect badly on the father who raised him and if Ham had been cursed then only Noah was truly at fault. But Canaan was an innocent. He wasn't responsible for Noah getting drunk on the wine he made by his own hand, so filthy stinking drunk that he stripped off his clothes before falling into a stupor. Ham merely came upon the old codger, passed out in his own vomit, and then hurried to tell his brothers, Japheth and Shem, that the old fart was in the bottle again. So warned, they covered their old man without seeing him in his altogether, and for that they got blessings. But poor Ham, just trying to get shit together after all the mess of the flood and put things right didn't have any such warning and it was as much a surprise to him as it was to Noah to see the old fool like that. There isn't anything more ornery than an old man with a hangover, particularly one who regularly talks to God Almighty and can count on the Big Guy to back him up.

But the rap Noah laid on Canaan was the first of a long line of Cover-Your-Ass bullshit to be visited on the heads of innocents. Because of it, Black folk have been demonized, denigrated, defiled, desecrated, dismembered, disenfranchised, dishonored, dismissed and generally dissed by every race descended from Japheth and Shem, which pretty much includes everybody not Black or dark skinned. Yeah, Antipas knew all about the use of Noah's curse to justify the conquest of the New World and the colonization of Africa and the sending of pious missionaries to take the gospel to the heathens while plundering their lands. No matter that Black folk have nonetheless excelled at everything they touched and that they have survived the worst that mankind could throw at them and still stand tall and proud. None of what good Black people have accomplished matters. All the world wants to see is a nigga in a doo-rag dropping dimes on shorties, selling crack on the corner and spittin' rhymes with dat flow dat dey do so well, passin' the ball to Lebron, hittin' Terrell in the end zone, tap tap tappin' that ole soft shoe and doin' that jive shit that's sure to be the hottest thing for young white kids in the 'burbs next season at the local mall by way of BET's *106 & Park*.

The world wants its niggas commoditized and deracinated so that it can assuage its pent up desire to be Black without all the negative bullshit that goes with it. They want to celebrate the exotic sensuality and jigaboo carnality of the Black woman while secretly lusting for the mythologized big black monster dick that they are still afraid of and driven to incarceration, emasculation, and miscegenation in an effort to tame that dick instead of their desires for it. Hell even the Japanese are sporting dreadlocks these days, how whacked is that? Everybody wants to be Black, because it smacks of some kind of coolness that defies ordinary non-Black folk, because we got that zing, you know, that ineffable something that just makes us shine hotter than all the rest and everybody else wants a piece of it, except real Black folk, who know that being Black hasn't been the joy ride that others are making of it at their expense. Then too, with 75% of Black folk, in the States at least, living well above poverty level, not knowing the inside of a ghetto because they have never lived in one, with solid middle and upper middle class values and kids who excel in school and go to college and get degrees and nice jobs and who have a nice home, well quite frankly they aren't considered true Blacks, not by Madison Avenue who only wants to sell Black Style, which they equate with fetishized urban ghettos; nor by Ghetto Fabulous Blacks, who don't want their promising rap careers to be jeopardized by the notion that not all Black people have it tough and do drugs to keep they sanity.

The sons of Japheth are still fanning the flames of that Curse to maintain their unassailable hegemony and keep a clean conscious about the evil they perpetuate. It is ironic how the forces that are hell bent on the destruction of the Black male and all that he represents are so ably assisted in their mission by the very people they want to eliminate. In a marriage of convenience made in Hell, the Japhethites and their punk ghetto bitches have succeeded in undoing in one generation all the work of Sister Sojourner, Brother Douglass, Booker T. and Father Du Bois, Countie, Zora, Langston and their fellow Niggeratti to elevate the image, the imagination and the potential of Black people in this world. Now, Destiny can pine for a soldier who's ghetto and has street cred, preferring a thug with a rap sheet and a hustle over a young Black man with a diploma and a career. It suits Them just fine to have the lowest amongst us stand in to represent us all, since it massages Their insecurities over Their supposed superiority. And if all else fails, they'll just get new niggas to take our place, hopefully without the surly attitude, unreliability around issues of time and the constant jonesin' for white pussy, like maybe some hard-working Guatemalans, Ecuadorians or Hondurans, since the Mexicans have been spoiled by too many years in confinement with us Blacks.

Damn that fucking bastard Noah, for spinning the heinousness which has made being Black a bigger cross to bear than the one the Lord carried to Golgotha. Damn the fucking bastard children of Japheth, sticking their noses into the tents of Shem and riding roughshod over the world like it was given to them as a divine right, enslaving all of the children of Noah save for their own and making such a mess of this world that it wouldn't be surprising if God just obliterated it again to spite them. Why else are we sitting on the verge of Ahriman the Great Satan being let loose a little season once more? Maybe Noah knew it all along and just wanted to make sure that Canaan would be there to clean up things again, after Japheth and Shem shat their pants, just like those faceless Black mammies wiping the asses of their white charges down in Brooklyn's Park Slope or on genteel Cambridge's Memorial Drive or in the shade of the Santa Monica high rises on Wilshire Boulevard where it meets the Pacific. Antipas' mind raced over these thoughts as he let Rocky's words echo in his ears. Descendant of Ham. Indeed!

"You're only partially right, Professor," Rocky gently scolded, interrupting Antipas' reverie, which reminded him again of the strong psychic powers the major possessed.

"While it's true that much evil has justified its existence on the basis of Noah's regrettable choice of words, nonetheless the fact of the matter remains that the line of Ham has been the backbone of creation. We have not blown ourselves to bits and we have, however reluctantly, come to champion freedom over oppression, albeit politically if not economically, and we have the descendants of Ham to thank for that. I think the Japhethites are just a little slow witted, but eventually, they'll get to where you and I already are, my good Doctor. They all evolve into their divine potential eventually, with strong guidance." Then the Major grinned broadly, flashing his perfect smile.

"Touche, Rocky," Antipas responded telepathically, allowing for the possibility that Rocky was indeed one of the so-called "good guys," a white-hat team player, his Café au Lait complexion notwithstanding, and in the trials ahead he would indeed be riding shotgun alongside Antipas and Hanna. At any rate, Antipas certainly hoped that would be the case, since he surmised there was a long, hard road ahead of them and the more hands pulling the better it would be for all concerned.

The Major started to laugh heartily.

At that, Antipas relaxed and a smile crept across his face and the two of them settled down into a mute communiqué between themselves, one psychic master to another. Hanna watched the exchange between Antipas and Rocky in silence, surreptitiously reading their thoughts. She smiled as the two men developed a strong rapport.

"Good," she thought to herself with satisfaction. "They're going to need that bond between them. Thank God Tip is on good behavior!"

At that last thought, both Antipas, his eyebrows lifted in mock surprise, and Rocky, smirking good-naturedly, suddenly turned to look at Hanna. Somewhat startled by their sudden attention, she realized that she had inadvertently let on that she had been following their psychic communique and let loose a demur smile at having been found out.

"Well if you two are ready, shall we get down to the business at hand?" Hanna cajoled, brushing off any embarrassment, as Rocky and Antipas both broke out in mirthful laughter. "We have some very anxious people across the hall waiting for us, somewhat impatiently I might add."

"I see we'll have to keep a sharp eye on that one," Rocky whispered aloud, conspiratorially, to Antipas.

"I'm afraid it's far too late for that now," Antipas replied, smiling at Hanna. "The game's a foot and she's on to us!"

"That'll be enough of that!" Hanna chortled, as she once again signaled to Rocky.

With a flourish, Rocky pulled some additional papers from his folio and handed copies to Hanna and Antipas. As Rocky began his briefing, Antipas carefully scanned the document in his hands, keeping one ear focused on the Major's words as his mind processed the information in front of him. It was an executive summary and the first line told Antipas all he needed to know about the task to which he had been summoned by Graciella's edict. The forces of Ahriman had breached no less than twenty of the thirty-three Gates Between the Worlds of spirit and flesh. Every major continent had at least three different vectors through which the forces of darkness were poised to strike. Massive numbers of demonic beings were gathering behind the compromised gates and, with the able assistance of human fellow-travelers paving the way for them, ready to attack every major population center on the planet, with extremely heavy concentrations targeting the world's key capitals. It was nothing less than Armageddon, cocked and ready to explode, and all that stood in the way was a suicidal plot cooked up by PsyOps to trip the inevitable prematurely and thus hope to catch the forces of darkness while they were still massed in their bunkers waiting for their orders from their Supreme Commander Ornias, who was presumed to have succeeded Ahriman. Central to the plan was one Antipas Pergamos, whose task was to infiltrate the Demonic High Command and, as the Major so eloquently phrased it, 'decapitate the snake as it was still poised to strike.'

Naturally, this being PsyOps, there was undoubtedly a parallel mission already in the works, led by another sacrificial fool, as Antipas called him, with capabilities similar to his own. Hanna was to be the observer on his own mission, while Rocky was to be his designated second. The only thing left out of the plan, Antipas felt, was any suggestion that he himself would survive the successful…decapitation. Considering the odds, PsyOps evidently wasn't counting on such an outcome. And why should they? They were actually serious in believing that some stranger could walk into the inner circle of Hell itself and get close enough to the top echelon of Satan's army to actually take them all out, annihilate them, and then fend for himself in the aftermath. Antipas shuddered at the thought of that.

"Now, now my good man," Rocky interrupted, "let's not get too far ahead of ourselves. Your unique qualifications as a Cambion and a Soul Eater will go a long way toward getting you inside the viper's nest, so to speak."

"Really? How can you be so sure of that," Antipas asked, his voice rising testily.

Rocky looked sternly at him. His eyes narrowed into tight slits and Antipas could feel a strong beam of intense energy boring into him.

"Come, now Professor Pergamos," the Major uttered in a voice so cold that the air around Antipas took on a definite chill. "Please don't play coy with us. Everyone here is keenly aware of what happened on the Carstensz Summit Ridge in Irian Jaya. According to our intelligence sources, which have been reliably confirmed at great sacrifice, you are considered something of a hero in Ahriman's High Command. The Archangel Berith himself personally credits the success of his operation directly to your intervention…or lack thereof. Your coming to them now, in the familiar role of traitor to your compatriots, will get you in the door, of that there is no question. That's why you were invited to the gathering at Esh Shabauk, they felt you were one of their own. That you are a traitor is not the issue. What is in doubt, my dear Professor, is whether you are indeed a traitor to *US* or not. And let me assure you, if you are, I can personally promise that regardless of whatever pleasantries those demons might mete out to your miserable soul in the event they unmask your mission, Yahweh's punishment will be infinitely worse! Far worse. Do I make myself clear, Professor?"

Antipas looked Rocky squarely in the eyes and held his gaze with a smoldering glare. Despite the smile frozen insincerely on his otherwise passive face, he reeled from the sudden shift in the Major's demeanor. Gone was the veneer of social courtesy, replaced now with a harsher, reál politique whose clearly defined boundaries enclosed sharply edged distinctions in black and white. So that was their little game, he thought deeply to himself, well below the perceptive frequencies of his telepathic compatriots. This whole PsyOps mission was a clever little ruse to exact retribution for his perceived failings at Irian Jaya and Esh Shabauk. If he went through with it as a game little soldier, the Demon were sure to discover his real purpose and damn him to an excruciating fate of depraved torture, which Yahweh would undoubtedly intercede in at some convenient point of His choosing after sufficient punishment had been inflicted and grant him eternal life in the Elysian Fields. However, if he refused or failed to carry out his end of the deal, then Yahweh would shred him in a rain of hellfire that would make the demons' torments seem mild by comparison. Either way, Antipas reasoned, he was going to experience one hellaciously painful demise. He was, as it were, damned if he did and damned if he didn't. A dilemma indeed and one that would require the most delicate of calculations if he were to succeed in escaping both potentials for near certain death. The deck was certainly stacked against him.

"I don't particularly like those odds, Rocky," Antipas said out loud at last, sounding chillingly cheerful, "But under the circumstances, my dear Major, I guess they'll have to do."

"Good!" Rocky said with a shout, slapping the palms of his hands on the folio in his lap, his mood returning to its previous good-naturedness. "I'm glad we have arrived at this little understanding. Now then, shall we see what our guests across the hallway are up to?"

Hanna, who had been silently observing Antipas as the Major spoke, released a small tight smile of relief. She had been clearly worried about how Antipas would take the harsh message delivered by the Major. Antipas gave her a brief glance, his eyes shining brightly, with an all too familiar flicker of devious insurrection lurking just below the surface. She knew at that keeping his mercurial personality focused on the task at hand would be a major challenge and that glance told her that if she had any thoughts of things going smoothly, she could throw them out the window. You just don't keep an eleventh degree initiate of the Ordo Templi Orientis on a tight leash. This was going to be a very bumpy ride, she thought. And as Antipas followed after the Major he elaborately crossed his fingers behind his back in a manner specifically designed to get her attention. Hanna shook her head as she smiled, despite herself.

"A very bumpy ride indeed," she thought silently, as the Major rapped politely on the door of the next room.

7 – THE GAME BEGINS

The three entities waiting for them in the room across the hallway were in a totally disagreeable humor, partially on account of their having had to wait for Antipas and his party to finally arrive, but mostly because it was just the nature of their being. The nasty row that Antipas had overheard when he was searching for Hanna seemed to still permeate the air and two of the beings made a distinct point of keeping their distance from the third. This latter one, a huge, corpulent figure whose grotesque weight deformed his features and made his speech slow and heavy, was clearly the leader of the evil little cabal. He positively reeked of sulfur and brimstone, leaving no doubt as to his recent origins. But most interesting to Antipas was the way this enormous being radiated an undercurrent of latent potency and strong occult power. It surrounded him like a dark halo. Oh, and speaking of darkness, these three entities were the blackest beings that Antipas had ever encountered. Next to them a lump of coal looked like snow on an asphalt driveway in winter. Whatever light shone in the room was swallowed up in the blackness of their skin like stars colliding with a black hole in space. He knew instantly that these three would play starring roles in the drama that was unfolding. And as if on cue, the big entity stood up with a gracefulness that belied his enormous size and extended a huge hand toward Antipas.

"Professor Pergamos, I presume?" he said in a smooth baritone voice that was unctuously pleasant. "It is an honor to meet you at last, sir."

Antipas reached out and shook the fat entity's hand. His palm was searing hot and oily and he held Antipas' hand in a very firm grasp for a long while that bordered on the uncomfortable. Antipas could tell he was being evaluated by the fat being, as if he were somehow reading Antipas through the pores of his own skin. It made his flesh crawl but he was careful to avoid giving away too much while the entity probed him.

"I have waited a long time for the pleasure of this moment," the fat being announced, still firmly holding onto Antipas' hand.

"Well I hope it won't be a disappointment for you then," Antipas replied without emotion. "You know how anticipation can sometimes inflate things."

"Oh come now, Professor!" the fat being chortled, "We are far from disappointed. It is indeed a pleasure!"

"You're too kind, er, ah…" Antipas rejoined, raising his eyebrow slightly.

"Ah, yes, Professor, forgive my lack of manners. The name's Dieter."

"Mr. Dieter. No last name?"

"Harumph! Harumph!" the fat being laughed extravagantly.

"In Jordan, all roads lead to Amman," Hanna interjected, "And in Amman, all roads lead to simply Dieter."

"Well said!" Dieter exclaimed, looking at Hanna with a salacious grin that stirred a little jealous antipathy within Antipas. "Well said, indeed Madame Minister!"

Rocky efficiently took command of the conversation.

"I've given the good professor a brief overview of matters as they stand currently, but perhaps you might be gracious enough to provide him with your perspective, Monsieur Dieter?"

Dieter turned swiftly toward the Major and gave him a cursory nod of acknowledgement. Antipas thought he detected some slight hostility between the two, but quickly brushed it aside as the fat being started to speak.

"Harumph!" he snorted, "quite right my dear Major, after all, time is running out."

With an elaborate flourish, Dieter seated himself on a small sofa, taking up the entire thing with his enormous bulk. He fished inside the inner breast pocket of his coat, made of an unknown but exquisite material that flowed naturally with his every movement and which gave him a very distinguished, almost magisterial air, before pulling out a large, elegantly slim cigar.

"Mind if I smoke?" he asked perfunctorily, looking around at the assembled company. Without waiting for any possibility of objection, he lit the cigar and took a few puffs. The aroma was sweet, even a little hypnotic, especially when combined with his deep sonorous voice, modulated to a light monotone that gave full effect to his words. Seeing Antipas staring at him critically, Dieter smiled, flashing a sharp set of ragged black teeth set in blood red gums.

"Would you care to join me, Professor?"

"I don't ordinarily indulge, but under the circumstances that sounds like a capital idea," Antipas demurely replied. "That aroma is most unusual. I can't quite place it."

"It's a very special blend of my own concoction. Far better than any Cuban or Dominican imposter you're likely to find. Here…" he said, handing Antipas a fresh cigar.

Antipas held the long slim shaft to his nose, inhaling the sweet aroma of its wrapper.

"I have a very simple rule, Professor," Dieter began. "Never trust a man who doesn't smoke, drink or fornicate. I detest a man without vices. It means he has far too high an opinion of himself to be worth a damn. Show me a man who knows intimately the frailty of his flesh and I'll show you a true saint. Harumph! Harumph!"

"Well I suppose that just about covers all of my failings," Antipas replied jovially, drawing deeply on the cigar and exhaling a series of perfect smoke rings into the space above Dieter's head.

The effect of the cigar was indeed powerful, almost hallucinogenic, and Antipas found himself struggling to stay focused on Dieter's words as he launched into his monologue. From time to time, one or the other of his two compatriots would make some sharp snort after Dieter had made a point, which brought a swift chilling look from him that must have had a particularly strong negative psychic impact, since the offending being immediately winced or yelped with pain and slunk further into another corner of the room as far away from him as was possible. The basic message that Dieter imparted was that he was very high up in the good graces of the demons' central command. It turned out that Dieter was a dealer in occult armaments of an especially lethal variety and that had earned him his place of vaunted esteem in the Demonic Realms. But he was also a realist and knew that the ensuing clash between the forces of darkness and the celestial hordes would create enormous opportunities for enterprising gentlemen such as himself, who weren't too picky about which side eventually won, as long as they were on the prevailing side. By placing his bets evenly between both sides,

Dieter hoped to profit handsomely in the end. Profit aside, he also had some personal scores to settle with certain members of the High Command who had offended him in front of Ornias, who had become the principal leader following Ahriman's assassination. The offense had caused Dieter some great personal loss which he was very keen to exact vengeance for. Somehow, the presumed female of the two other entities with him was somehow connected to that offense and a constant reminder of the pain of it. Antipas couldn't really figure that part out since his head was reeling in and out of consciousness from the smoke and taste of the cigar. Dieter kept a close watch on Antipas' face as he spoke, nodding his head hypnotically every time he caught Antipas' eye.

"How are you enjoying the cigar my dear Professor?" Dieter asked him at one point.

Antipas struggled to make a reply, but could only nod his head and grin like a damn fool. Deep down, he kept reminding himself that Dieter and his companions were not to be trusted. In fact, from this point on, there was only one person that Antipas could trust, and that was himself, and even then....

"Personally, I like my cigars like I like my men," Dieter grinned lasciviously as he wickedly winked at Antipas, leaving no doubt as to his interests. "The darker the wrapper, the sweeter the taste! Harumph! Harumph!"

Dieter resumed his monologue as Antipas exerted even greater effort to counter the effects of the cigar. He knew it was some form of mind control that Dieter was trying to capture him with and while he wanted Dieter to think that he was in fact succeeding, Antipas desperately wanted only the mere appearance of the thing, not the actual fact of it. There was too much at stake for him to succumb to some cheap magic trick from a fat devil only hours out of Hell. So Antipas smiled once again, playing the fool, and tried to listen carefully to Dieter's words while measuring them against his actions.

"I've got your number, fatso," Antipas thought deeply to himself. He knew that if he had to, he could use Dieter's obvious fixation with him to his own advantage at the right time and under the right circumstances. "One doesn't get to be an eleventh-degree initiate of O.T.O. without learning to play all sides of the ball," Antipas mused silently.

"You know, Professor," Dieter offered grandly, taking a long draw on his cigar, "I have one other simple rule: The only man worth trusting is the man whose sole focus is his own self-interest. A man will lie about everything else, but if his self-interest is at stake, he'll defy Heaven and Hell to get what he wants. That's something I can work with. How about you, Professor Pergamos? What do you think?"

"I couldn't agree more with your assessment," Antipas offered cheerfully, relieved that he was beginning to hold his own against the insidious magic of Dieter's cigar and secure in the knowledge that Dieter had not read his thoughts, nor did he have any idea of just how close to the mark he had come.

Indeed, Antipas reasoned, one can control another through his appetites – be they lusts for money, sex, power or what have you. But you can own another being entirely if you can stand on the threshold between them and that which their innermost soul desires. The trick is to be seen as the gateway through which those desires can be realized, and not as an obstacle that must be removed. That was certainly a point of reference that Antipas and Dieter shared completely. From Antipas' perspective, however, he wasn't convinced that Dieter had indeed been fully forthcoming in his little sob story as to why he was now willing to work so closely with PsyOps and help them in the plot to decapitate the Demonic High Command. "He's lying," Antipas thought in the deepest recesses of his mind. What was Dieter *really* after? That was the burning question that Antipas most wanted to know the answer to. And whatever the answer, it would be the critical variable in whether or not his mission would in fact succeed. He looked at the two other entities, now huddled together conspiratorially in a far corner, deeply engaged in an animated conversation. "Those two might be helpful," Antipas concluded, noting how they had reacted upon seeing the dark red plume above his head. "At pain of losing their souls, they might be very helpful indeed."

Dieter, meanwhile, finally laid out his concept for the next phase of the game. The plan was to move their base of operations closer to the Gate of ADAR, to a small settlement called Ba'ir a few hours northeast of Esh Shabauk, where they could make contact with an ultra-elite squadron of Archons who controlled all access to the immediate environs of the Gate. Everything would depend on how they were brought into the Archon's command headquarters. If they could successfully make it past the guards, who were personally chosen for their mission by Berith, the second highest Archangel in Ornias' inner circle, then they had a chance of achieving their ultimate objective. It would be necessary for them to spend an extended time ingratiating themselves with both the Archons, who were a notoriously mistrustful lot and gifted with extremely potent occult powers to boot, in addition to the next several ranks up the command chain, comprised of even more deadly and powerful corrupted angelic forces, before they could hope to have an audience with the uppermost echelons, maybe even with Berith or Ornias personally. Antipas would need an airtight cover story that would allay their natural suspicions as to his motives and that story would have to be deeply ingrained in his psyche, since the demons would probe him much more closely than Dieter had when they shook hands. Hanna and Rocky would likewise need plausible raison d'êtra for their presence as well.

They would leave at midnight that very night and camp in the desert during the day, in order to arrive at Ba'ir under cover of darkness, where they would be met by one of Dieter's associates. Dieter would provide the necessary accoutrements for their journey. Satisfied by the reaction to his grand scheme, Dieter elevated his improbable bulk from the sofa with considerable grace and ambled over to the Major.

"Well Rocky, looks just like the old days once again, only this time it's you and me against the world instead of each other, eh?" Dieter purred in his most oleaginous fashion as he shook hands with Rocky.

"Indeed and let's hope that, unlike in the old days, we are on the winning side *together* for once!"

"Well said, Major! Well said!"

Dieter then made a flamboyant gesture of kissing Hanna's hand, despite her obvious disgust at the creepiness of his manner.

"Madam Minister, it has been an inestimable pleasure. I so look forward to our time together with great anticipation! You know, the desert can be a cold place at night. It helps to have close friends around to share their body heat! Harumph! Harumph!"

As Dieter turned to Antipas, his eyes on fire, his face once again broke out into a wicked grin. He grasped Antipas' hand and held it for a long while.

"I do hope, my dear Professor, that we come to be *very* good friends." Dieter said aloud. Pulling Antipas slightly out of earshot of Hanna and Rocky, he continued in a barely audible whisper. "When all this unpleasantness is over, we should talk about a longer term collaboration. I think we could make great profit together, you and me. Oh, and here, have another cigar, to commemorate our burgeoning partnership."

He winked at Antipas with a most prurient glee while extending the gift to Antipas and then abruptly turned away before Antipas could reply. Dieter snapped sharply at the other two entities in a very rare and ancient language that was nonetheless familiar to Antipas from his research and they followed him out of the room in a great sulk. Once Dieter and his entourage had left, Rocky made the obvious observation:

"Well, that was a bastardly lot! I don't trust that despicable, fat son-of-a-bitch in any way, shape or form. But on the other hand… he has unparalleled access to the very highest levels of the demon's senior command and if he can get us inside, as he indicated, then that alone is worth the gamble. Any other alternative would take considerably more time to develop and frankly we just don't have that luxury."

"I'm more concerned about what he may already have said to Ornias' people. I feel like we're being played for fools, walking blindly into some kind of trap," Hanna sighed wearily. She looked carefully at Antipas, her feelings for him written all over her face. "Most of all, I'm deathly afraid for your safety, Tip. There's no telling what will happen to you once you do get into the upper echelons of the High Command."

Antipas took a moment to reflect before responding, inhaling the sweet aroma of Dieter's cigar while keenly aware that both Hanna and the Major were anxiously awaiting his evaluation of the situation. He decided to let them wait since only moments before they were both pressing upon him the fact that he was to be the sacrificial lamb in mankind's quest to forestall Armageddon or face the wrath of Yahweh if he failed to take up his assigned cross to bear. As distasteful a creature as Dieter evidently was, there was still some virtue in what he said. He and Antipas could indeed make for a profitable partnership post-Apocalypse…at the very least, Dieter was the only entity so far, from either side, who even held out the remote possibility that there would indeed be a post-Apocalyptic future for one Antipas Pergamos. That alone was worth the price of admission to the game in his mind. Still savoring the unlit cigar, Antipas looked first at Hanna and then Rocky.

"It's been said that a long journey begins with a single step. We won't know what we'll find along the way until we actually stumble upon it. So I guess we'll just have to keep our own counsel close to the vest and see where Dieter eventually leads us." Smiling, Antipas slipped the cigar into a pocket of his jacket.

"And if nothing else, he sure has some of the best damn cigars I've ever experienced. That's enough of an inducement for me at the moment," he laughed heartily.

"Well then, I guess we better complete our preparations. We have a lot to do if we are to leave at midnight. Shall we rendezvous here at eleven-thirty then?" Rocky remarked brusquely, ignoring Antipas' attempted levity.

"I don't have a problem with that," Hanna replied, her voice twisted with conflicted emotions. "How about you, Tip?"

"I'll be ready," Antipas smirked, looking at Rocky and Hanna in a new light, his mind already busy with plans within plans as he contemplated the myriad potential paths radiating outward from the present moment. There were indeed potentialities ahead that offered real glimmers of hope for him personally and these were of particular interest. No road would be easy, but that was beside the point. His own survival was his paramount interest and he knew that Dieter had already ferreted that out. He would have to be on his best game if he wasn't to fall prey to any of Dieter's multitude of tricks. That fat demon would love nothing better than to have a Soul Eater at his personal beck and call. As the Major and Hanna exchanged some last minute pleasantries, Antipas also noted that he would have to maintain a charade of sincerity to their cause in order to keep them off his trail and maintain optimal maneuvering room to effect his own plans. Hanna would be easy enough, he calculated, already contemplating that some torrid sex would probably suffice. But Rocky was a more difficult proposition. "That one will require a bit of work," he smiled. "God how I do love a challenge," he mused silently.

As they drove back to Antipas' hotel, Hanna was mostly quiet. Gone was the fiery hellion racing through the chaos of Amman's traffic. She was much more pensive now, reserved even. Antipas stared at her profile, still as stunning as the first time he had met her. He felt a stirring in his pants. There was just no denying it, Hanna was one incredible beauty and the fact that she would deign to grace his homely countenance with her presence was still a source of wonderment to him. There was something else stirring in him, Antipas felt, a feeling that he had long ago given up any hope of ever being struck by. He shuddered involuntarily for a moment.

"Are you okay, Tip?" Hanna inquired sweetly, her voice an undercurrent of concern mixed with dread and tempered by resignation.

"Yeah, I'm fine," he answered gently, while placing his hand on her thigh.

"Things will be happening pretty rapidly from here on."

"Yeah, I know."

"Tip…," she hesitated.

Antipas thought he knew what she was going to say and the emotions welling up within him startled him again, making him tremble. Hanna felt it, sensed it, and looked at him with a long glance, taking her eyes off the road. She gave him a wan smile and that one gesture seemed to speak all the words that dared not pass between them. He returned her smile and squeezed her thigh ever so gently. It was enough. She never finished her thought and Antipas never had to admit the truth of what was happening inside him. They pulled up to his hotel, both of them staring straight ahead into the middle distance, without uttering a word.

"I'll pick you up at eleven o'clock sharp. Don't be late," Hanna said, speaking fast.

"I'll be ready," Antipas answered as he slipped out of the passenger side door, and slammed it shut. He turned to walk up the stairs of the hotel.

"Tip!," Hanna yelled from inside the car.

Antipas turned around to see her face engulfed in a broad playful grin.

"Pack light this time, okay? There'll be three of us with gear and I don't want you hogging up the place!"

Antipas smiled broadly and flashed an upturned thumb. Hanna honked the horn and drove off in a flurry of squealing rubber and flying gravel. He watched her speed away and just as he turned again to continue up the stairs, he noticed a familiar figure waiting across the street from the hotel, trying to be inconspicuous. Antipas smiled again and headed back down the stairs, walking straight toward his shadowy nemesis. It was at that moment that the hunger which had been slowly building up in him erupted with fervent urgency. "Come into my parlor, my little fly" Antipas thought to himself. "It's been a long hard day and daddy's oh so very hungry."

8 – MARTYRS AND SAINTS

Mehkmed slept fitfully, tossing and turning until he was wet with sweat, before finally coming to rest, spread-eagle on his back, exhausted. For the last few weeks, his sleep had been disturbed by the same dream. In the beginning, he was titillated by it, since there was a streak of submissiveness deep inside him that only a few had successfully teased him into exhibiting. But after a while the dream began to frighten him, as if it were a warning of the punishments that awaited him in the hereafter for the sin of being a sodomite.

In the dream, Mehkmed's long skinny body is naked as he hangs by the thumbs from a scaffold in the middle of a dusty public square, crowded with throngs of onlookers staring at him. He can feel their eyes exploring every centimeter of his light mocha skin, with its thick mat of soft, dark hair heavily knotted by streaks of sweat and blood from the beating given him by the guards who accosted him in the middle of the previous night. Mehkmed knows he is handsome; his dark good looks have intrigued both men and women on many continents, though curiously it is the men that seem to fall especially hard for him more often than not. Even now, hanging naked in this square, he can see the familiar look of desire in the eyes of those closest to him, along with telltale indications of a healthy boner tenting some robes here and there.

As the crowd shrieks, taunts and hurls curses at him, five huge men appear, wearing black hoods that cover their faces save for only the most minimal slit for their glaring eyes, and leather harnesses that cross their chests in a Y, with the tail of the Y snaking down their ripped abs and disappearing into tight leather shorts snugly holding the massive bulges protruding from their crotches. They march through the unruly mob and take up position around Mehkmed in a circle. Each man holds a long cat-o-nine tails in his powerful hands. The sight of these half-naked men in black leather causes Mehkmed to become aroused and his erection drives the crowds even wilder and forces the hitherto unseen police to rush in and force them back to the edges of the square. The officers link arms and create a bulwark between him and the frenzied mob.

Then, the five men begin to whip Mehkmed's defenseless body from the neck down, slowly at first then increasing in intensity until the cat-o-nine tails begin to break his skin with each stinging blow. Mehkmed is powerless to prevent the lashes from landing on his exposed flesh, his private parts and ass finding special favor from his tormentors. Soon, his body is covered in blood and the pain is so intense, Mehkmed prays for unconsciousness. Then suddenly, the whipping stops, the group of men steps back a few paces and five women rush up to Mehkmed's flayed body and throw salt on him, causing him unbearable agony as they vigorously rub the salt into the open wounds, taking particular relish in packing the salt around his balls and foreskin. The women are chased away by another group of five men who climb up onto the scaffold and then piss on Mehkmed from above, their urine creating an excruciating acid that burns the raw edges of his wounds as it mixes with the salt. When they're done, the five half-naked men return to their positions and start whipping him with renewed fury.

Mehkmed never knew how the dream ended, because by the time his pain reached its maximum he awoke, as now, to the familiar feeling of his beloved Jamal's firm round butt grinding against him, ravenously hungering to be impaled by Mehkmed's throbbing member. As he slowly opens his eyes, completing the transition from the dream-space into the reality of the present moment, Mehkmed sees Jamal's smooth blue-black cheeks slide up and down his dark brown shaft. After a few powerful strokes, Mehkmed is on the verge of exploding, but the talented Jamal, feeling the pressure building in the veins of Mehkmed's balls, lifts himself off his beloved, turns around, grabs Mehkmed's legs and lifts them, exposing Mehkmed's naked defenseless ass. Without any hesitation, Jamal thrusts his enormous black snake full bore into Mehkmed and plows him in long, deep strokes from the tip of his shaft to the base of his balls. Mehkmed looks into Jamal's chiseled face, sweat dripping off the straight angles of his chin.

"What a handsome devil," Mehkmed thinks to himself, his eyes rolling backward as Jamal's vigorous thrusting propels him into an ecstatic revelry.

Mehkmed's mind flows back to the first time he and Jamal met. He was on an extremely rare summer holiday from his job as a floor runner on the New York Stock Exchange, soaking up some of the local color on the balcony of the St. Barth's Beach Hotel, overlooking the celebrity-filled playground of the ultra-haute Guanahani Hotel and Spa just a short stroll down the Anse de Toiny. Jamal, who had grown up on the island but now lived in New York and worked coincidentally as a broker for a major specialist firm on Wall Street, was with a mixed group of cool local buddies and fish-out-of-water New Yorkers trying very hard to impress the locals, including a pretty light-skinned Bajan girl from Queens who tried everything to keep and hold his roving attention. But Jamal's eyes, which had riveted on Mehkmed as soon as he saw him, spoke volumes about his real interests. Jamal sauntered casually over to Mehkmed's table.

"Hey, what's up?" Jamal had asked in a sweet, friendly voice. "Wanna go to the beach with us?"

Mehkmed hesitated at first, making all sorts of excuses – he didn't have a bathing suit, he sunburned too easily, his lunch had just arrived – but finally relented after Jamal demolished every one of his defenses and eventually said okay. They all crowded into a couple of rickety mokes, one of the small makeshift utility vehicles that are a staple form of transportation on the island, and headed over to Grande Saline. As soon as they hit the beach, everyone in the group, including Jamal, began stripping off their clothes since unbeknownst to Mehkmed nudity was allowed with a wink and a nod by the locals at Grand Saline. The informal tradition was that if you were straight you headed off to the right and if you were gay you headed off to the left. Their little group went straight down the middle of the beach and encamped close to the water's edge. Mehkmed's eyes widened at the sight of Jamal's body, especially his enormous endowment. Jamal noticed Mehkmed's brazen stare and smiled slyly back at him, which caused Mehkmed no end of embarrassment after which he absolutely refused to undress since the tent at his crotch was too obvious a marker of his interest. Jamal teased him mercilessly, though subtly so as not to out him in front of the others in the group.

As Jamal and some of the guys played soccer on the edge of the surf, the Bajan girl with the eye for Jamal and perhaps feeling competition for his affections, snuck up behind Mehkmed and unceremoniously pulled his shorts down, exposing him for all to see. Her loud laughter drew the attention of the rest of the group and once again Mehkmed found himself embarrassed by his arousal, especially with Jamal staring right at him with that same sly smile on his face. Later, his "newbie" initiation complete and Mehkmed now as naked as the others, the group pretty much left him alone while they teamed up to play volleyball. That's when Jamal informed Mehkmed that there were some interesting petroglyphs on the rocks at the far end of the left side of the beach and offered to show them to him. Once they were out of sight of the group, Jamal grabbed Mehkmed by the hand, pulled him against his chest, and began kissing him passionately. They made love for the first time right there on the beach. Mehkmed had never experienced anything as tender and compassionate like sex with Jamal before and he was hooked. He and Jamal were together every day until Mehkmed had to return to New York. A week later, when his own holiday was over, Jamal joined Mehkmed there and they had been together ever since.

Mehkmed rolled his eyes deeper into his head, relishing the feel of Jamal's hard thrusts poking into his guts and taking his breath away with each jolt and he tried to open himself wider to accommodate him. The intensity of Jamal's thrusts increased and Mehkmed craned his neck to watch their reflection in the mirrored doors of the closet past the foot of the bed. The sight of his firm round hairy ass, with dimpled cheeks, the color of cinnamon, being wailed upon by Jamal's muscular Black body drove Mehkmed over the edge and he erupted in a massive orgasm. Jamal gripped Mehkmed's cheeks and drove as deeply as he could into Mehkmed's willing depths, bucking hard against Mehkmed's butt before finally collapsing on top of him, totally spent.

"Damn, that was a good fuck," Jamal hoarsely whispered after a short while, as he slipped out of Mehkmed and rolled onto his back.

Mehkmed slid onto his belly, gingerly trying to avoid the cold wetness of their commingled passions streaking the sheets. "Yeah, you dug it out real good, papi."

"Shit, it's nearly eight o'clock man, you're gonna be late for work," Jamal blurted out as he turned his head to check the time. He bolted upright and slapped Mehkmed sharply on the ass.

"Hey! What was that for?" Mehkmed yelled, trying to lift himself onto his elbows in a fleeting attempt to whack Jamal's perky behind before he left the bed.

"Just making sure I didn't pop those cute bubble cheeks when I was fucking the shit out of them. You know I can't stand a flabby ass", Jamal cracked as he tickled Mehkmed's feet before disappearing into the bathroom.

Mehkmed lay on the bed, letting the cool breeze wafting from the open window sooth his throbbing wet ass, which still reverberated from Jamal's piggish assault.

"I'm sure going to miss mornings like these," Mehkmed mused wistfully, wiggling his butt and deeply inhaling the musky funk of sweaty man-sex. The sound of Jamal's shower, combined with the thick humidity in the air and the distant roar of morning rush hour traffic twenty-three floors below on Central Park West, lulled Mehkmed into a meditative slumber. Though his eyes were closed, he was acutely aware of every sensation, from the tiny metallic click as the minutes rolled by on the clock by the bed, to the feeling of the billowy breeze on the wet, curly hairs of his balls. His thoughts flowed in slow regression back to the small dusty square of his dream. It looked hauntingly familiar, like a deeply suppressed memory from a long time ago, well before Mehkmed came to New York to pursue his career in finance, another lifetime before he even left his native Jordan. "Where have I seen that square?"

Then suddenly it came to him, it was his ancestral village of Ba'ir, situated on the banks of a seasonal river that washed down the rugged flanks of the Jabal Ithriyat mountains, in the middle of the Jordanian desert. He hadn't thought about his homeland in years, especially not the horrific memories of his early life in that forlorn rural village, but now all that came flowing back into his mind as vividly as the dream, but even more disturbingly because it was real once. Mehkmed had been very young when the extraordinarily tall men in black robes smelling of sulfur and rotting flesh strode into the village and rounded up his father and the other male elders and made them kneel down in a row in the middle of the square, where they were beheaded, one by one, in front of Mehkmed, his mother, his brothers and sisters and the rest of the village. The evil men then issued an ultimatum – accept Lord Ahriman as the One True God or join our fathers in death. Fearful for their lives, his mother and the remaining adults quickly paid obeisance to the Lord of the evil ones. Soon, more of the wicked men came, smelling just as vile and full of death as the first ones to arrive. They routinely beat and raped women and children, not even the few older males who survived the initial slaughter owing to their advanced age were immune.

Mehkmed, though only a child, nonetheless was singled out by the leader of the evil ones for particular favor, owing to his dark good looks. The pain of those cruel encounters was so severe that Mehkmed prayed for death almost every day. His cries and screams only seemed to goad the evil beast into even more depraved acts of wickedness at the expense of his young victim. As he grew older, Mehkmed came under the tutelage of one of the imams brought to the village by the evil ones. He quickly learned that by staying close to the imam he was subjected to fewer assaults from the evil brute who abused him. The imam evidently held a great deal of power over the members of the evil clan. So Mehkmed showed great devotion to the teachings of the imam, eventually becoming his star pupil and a trusted disciple. The imam taught him that the day was fast approaching when Lord Ahriman would once more be free to roam the regions of his earthly kingdom. Mehkmed, the imam had told him fervently in a moment of deep revelation after a sacred magical initiation that involved their own sexual union, had been chosen by Lord Ahriman himself to help prepare the way for his investiture. A great sacrifice would have to be made but in the end, Mehkmed would be rewarded with riches without measure and life everlasting.

It was heady stuff for a young, impressionable youth in the middle of an arid desert, surrounded by despicably evil throngs from another world who terrorized his people on a daily basis. Many years later, and a half a world away from his humble beginnings, Mehkmed was now on the verge of fulfilling the imam's fateful prophecy. He had excelled at his studies and was able to make his way to New York and obtain a coveted job working in the heart of Wall Street. As luck would have it, that very morning the bell on the NYSE was to be rung by one of the wealthiest men in the world, whose company was celebrating its anniversary as a public concern. A number of other powerful and important people would be joining him, including the governor, the mayor, the state's senior U.S. senator and a bevy of other public officials. If there was one day for the legions of Lord Ahriman to make a statement as to His imminent arrival, this was that day, Mehkmed thought. He had worked long and hard for just this moment, training himself to be able to fit the explosive device given to him by the imam deep inside his anal cavity, where it would be undetected by the security measures at the exchange. Jamal with his horse-hung endowment had certainly played a major role in Mehkmed's preparations, even if he was totally unaware of his contribution. Indeed, so had the two security guards who routinely manned the employees' entrance to the exchange, whom Mehkmed had befriended, enjoying regular trysts with them several times a day during breaks at work. The imam had said that such regular sexual activity was totally acceptable as long as it was in the pursuit of the higher aim of bringing jihad to the infidels. The evil beast who had first accosted him, whose name was Ornias, was the Great Lord Ahriman's most trusted and valued confidant and that too had marked Mehkmed as being particularly favored for this most important mission on behalf of his master.

Jamal came bounding out of the bathroom and French-kissed Mehkmed passionately before hurriedly dressing in one of the expensive bespoke suits made expressly for him by the same tailor used by the Prince of Wales.

"Hey, you *are* planning on going to work today aren't you?" Jamal playfully teased, as Mehkmed took one more languorous stretch in the middle of the bed. "The rent's due at the end of the week and I'm not covering for your share again no matter how much of that phat booty you serve up, okay? I want my money bitch!"

"I'm going, I'm going," Mehkmed replied with a yawn as he raised himself and sat on the edge of the bed.

He couldn't possibly explain to Jamal that unfortunately he would be covering the rent by himself for a long time to come and without the added bonus of Mehkmed's sexual favors. No, there would be no more time for such earthly pleasures. He had a mission of the utmost importance and today was the day of his transcendence into the mystical realms of the great paradise promised by Lord Ahriman to only his most loyal and devout followers.

"I'll call you about doing lunch later," Jamal yelled from the hallway, as he headed toward the front door of the apartment. "I've got a meeting with a big client in midtown but I should be free after one or so."

"Finally!" Mehkmed exhaled, hearing the echo of the door slamming shut. The clock read 8:30am. There was only an hour left. He hopped off the bed in a determined frenzy and rushed to the closet where he carefully removed a small trunk hidden in the far back corner under piles of winter clothes. He was happy that Jamal would be far away from the financial district this morning as he took out the sacred object that would soon announce the long prophesied arrival of Armageddon on earth. Mehkmed smiled.

"Damn the fucking dream," he hollered at the top of his lungs, "Praise Ahriman! Long may He reign on earth! Ahriman Akbar!"

* * *

Frank rushed into Gabriella's office in a cold sweat, not bothering to knock.

"It's on, chief!" he yelled as soon as he entered.

Gabriella quickly hung up the phone and folded her hands in front of her on top of the desk. She clearly had already gotten the psychic vibe well before he had heard from Joey.

"I just informed the President. He's on his way here since we can't trust the integrity of Iron Mountain under the current circumstances. Too close to the Yellowstone supervolcano, which is sure to be a likely target of the demon forces at some point."

"We've got to warn the authorities in New York City," Frank replied breathlessly.

"It's too late for that now, Frank," Gabriella sighed deeply. "Is Joey safe?"

"Yeah, he was already on his way upstate to his safe house in the Adirondacks when he called me," Frank responded, seating himself with a heavy thud on the sofa across from her desk. "How much time do they have?" he asked, his voice strained.

"We should start getting reports any moment. The casualties will be horrific, far worse than on September 11. Are there any PsyOps folks remaining in London, Frankfort, Dubai or the other financial hubs?"

"No, we moved them all out after Joey's report from the other day."

"Good." Gabriella was silent for a long while, staring into the middle distance, remotely viewing the carnage that was even then being unleashed by the forces of Ahriman all across the globe. The world found itself suddenly and shockingly engulfed in an ages old struggle that threatened the very survival of all its inhabitants.

"I pray to god Antipas comes through for us," she remarked at last. "If he doesn't, we're all doomed, Frank."

Frank looked squarely at her, returning her gaze.

"He'll come through, chief. We've got divine providence tipping the scales in our favor, remember?"

"Right," she replied, cracking a slight smile. "Our back-up insurance policy. Still, things would look a whole lot better if we knew Antipas would indeed succeed."

Frank nodded his head solemnly. As much as he personally disliked Antipas Pergamos, their fate and that of the rest of humanity now laid squarely on his slim shoulders. "Don't blow this you fucking prick," he thought to himself, not caring if Gabriella read his mind or not.

9 – DESERT ENCOUNTERS

The Humvee, driven with a single-minded determination bordering on the maniacal by one of Dieter's zombie hired hands, hit the great swell trailing after one monstrously huge sand dune that practically obliterated the road ahead for as far as the eye could see at breakneck speed, throwing Antipas hard against the headrest before pitching him forward so fast it nearly flipped him over the front seat, straight into Rocky's lap. Naturally, he alone of the four occupants crammed into the passenger compartments was the only one not fastened into his safety harness. The driver, who seemed to have left this plane of earthly existence some indeterminately long time ago, didn't count since he clearly was beyond such trivial concerns.

"You okay, Tip?" Hanna called out in his direction from the compartment directly behind the driver's, her voice taught with concern as he ricocheted to a sudden stop and slumped backward against the headrest in the compartment next to hers.

Antipas gingerly rubbed his neck and shoulders, wincing slightly, as he reeled from the rude awakening that had disturbed his otherwise surprisingly deep, meditative slumber. Satisfied that he was no worse for the wear, he shook himself like a wet dog emerging from a sudden and unwanted bath before responding.

"Yeah," Antipas replied ruefully, searching for the elusive buckles on the harness that he was now fixated on securing. "I'm still in one piece, after a fashion."

"I hope the same can still be said for our vehicle!" Rocky responded with a laugh, playing off the fact that the Humvee was a rather crude, ramshackle affair whose service life had long ago passed its expiration date too, not unlike its driver. He pointed toward the windshield.

"I think our destination is just up ahead. Could anyplace be more forsaken?"

The three of them stared in disbelief at the scene rapidly rolling into view in front of them. Illuminated by a nearly full moon so bright as to compete with the sun for bragging rights as to which was more radiant, the landscape looked to be straight out of Hell itself, with dark foreboding clouds hanging low over an endless stretch of barren sand that glowed like sulfur and had been blasted by incessant sirocco winds into fantastical, otherworldly shapes that looked as if they had been gouged out of solid amber. And despite the fact that the sun had been down for hours, it was hot, so hot that the oppressiveness of it leaked into the cabin of the Humvee as if it were an open convertible instead of a climate-controlled, armor-plated assault vehicle. There appeared to be no signs of life, no visible habitations, nothing at all to break the monotony of the bleak horizon in all directions, save for the dark jagged peaks of the Jabal Ithriyat mountains rising in long, saw-tooth procession to the east.

The plan had been to arrive under cover of darkness but apparently Dieter had forgotten to take into account the phases of the moon in his calculations. As a result, their arrival was perfectly obvious to any remotely observant sentinel of the evil hordes who made Ba'ir their command headquarters. Making matters worse, there appeared to be no sign of Dieter's accomplices, as also planned, and the idea of driving full tilt into the middle of enemy territory in plain sight was more than a little disturbing to Rocky and Hanna. Then, as if their collective suspicions had coalesced into a mirage of ill tidings, there appeared a sudden flash of light on the near horizon as a column of vehicles scurried at high speed in their direction.

"I think we're about to have company," Antipas whispered to Hanna, who seemed to be on edge ever since they had left Amman. "You think Dieter speaks their language?" he jovially whispered conspiratorially into Rocky's ear, unconcerned if the driver could hear him.

"Well if he doesn't then we're going to have to implement Plan B a lot sooner than I anticipated," Rocky responded with a short, strained laugh.

Antipas took note of the Major's worried tone, since it remained unspoken that in actuality there was no Plan B to fall back on. He peered searchingly at the column quickly advancing in their direction. Just then a loud cackle surged through the radio speaker on the Humvee's dashboard as Dieter's voice barked some unintelligible order to the driver, who nonetheless understood perfectly what he was being commanded to do. To their surprise, the driver gunned the Humvee's big engine and drove even faster directly toward the lead vehicle in the quickly approaching column. They were headed on a collision course.

"Hmmm, not exactly the choice I'd have made," Antipas remarked aloud, still somewhat giddy after his earlier jolting episode.

He surreptitiously projected his thoughts so as not to be detected by the driver as he probed the oncoming vehicles to ascertain who or what was hurtling toward them in apparent disregard for the impending crash that seemed to be almost certain to happen. He felt Hanna's mind also searching for clues and he squeezed her hand as reassurance. Together their combined psychic energies quickly determined that the oncoming vehicles were being driven by humans, beleaguered residents of Ba'ir, using the full moon to flee their oppressive captivity since the demons seemed to be otherwise occupied in saturnine festivities celebrating some major event which had evidently just occurred. Using an intimate psychic frequency that only they shared, Antipas and Hanna exchanged hurried thoughts as they randomly read deeper into the minds of the assorted collection of men, women and children in the oncoming phalanx. They were, to a person, absolutely traumatized by whatever it was they were willing to risk death to escape from. Their collective pain bodies projected far into the ether surrounding them and Hanna, being more sensitive to psychic energies, gripped Antipas' hand so tightly he felt she would crush his fingers. He saw what she was reacting to, as well, and the sheer horror of what the demons had unleashed on the poor inhabitants of Ba'ir made even his usually stone-cold Soul Eater heart ache with empathy.

They were now only a few hundred feet away from a direct collision when Antipas belatedly realized that the people in the convoy couldn't see the Humvee from hell bearing down on them. Dieter had used some kind of special camouflage that effectively hid their presence even at relatively close range. Acting on a similar flash of insight, Rocky lunged for the steering wheel, but the driver was not about to be deterred from his deadly course. He lashed out at the Major with a quick thrust of his thick muscular arm, revealing razor-sharp claws that protruded a good six inches from the tips of his gnarled fingers. In that instant, Antipas, with even faster reactions than the driver's, grabbed the pitch black plume arcing over the driver's head and snapped his soul clean out of his body, rendering him an oozing pile of twisted flesh and bone. Rocky, nearly blinded by the sudden explosion of the driver's body, which covered the whole front passenger compartment of the Humvee in a gelatinous residue of putrid slime that stank to high heaven, nonetheless managed to wrench the big steering wheel sharply to avoid a head-on impact at the very last possible second.

Still traveling at a very high rate of speed, the Humvee veered wildly into the path of the vehicle Dieter was riding in, which had been making a beeline to impact the middle of the fleeing caravan. The horrific crash struck the Humvee directly in the driver's side door, which would have certainly killed the driver on impact if he had still been among the living. Hanna and Rocky, securely strapped into their jump seats, were thrashed around violently, but otherwise no worse for the ordeal. Antipas, having slipped out of his harness and elevated himself slightly above his seat to ride out the impact unscathed, sensed that the collision would make for good cover and surreptitiously wiped both Hanna's and the Major's memories of his having taken the soul of the driver. It was a very risky trick to pull on initiated Master Adepts like Hanna and Rocky. He had learned the technique from an indigenous sadhu during his brief time in Irian Jaya but had never had occasion to use it until now. Moreover, it was strictly a one-trick pony since a Master Adept's etheric body creates an Akashic record of their body's experiences in this plane and his or her finely attuned mind quickly learns to recognize the psychic dissonance of the memory lapse and thus prevent a second occurrence. Still, Antipas felt it was worth the risk under the present circumstances, since it was even rarer that anyone other than another Soul Eater should witness a soul being taken from its host. Souls have a nasty habit of attaching themselves at the cellular level to the bodies of their hosts, which makes the process of detaching them a particularly gruesome affair under the best of circumstances and certainly not for the faint of heart.

Now at least, with the driver's compartment totally mangled in the collision, it would appear as if the driver had died…or rather, returned to his previously dead state…as a result of the crash and not because he had been the unfortunate victim of a Soul Eater. And to make the ruse even more believable, Antipas restrained himself from devouring the recently detached soul despite the ravenous cravings of his stomach and propelled it at lightning speed in a direction opposite that of the fleeing caravan, now receding past the horizon and well out of sight. He knew that the presence of a fresh soul by itself would attract exactly the kind of unwanted attention that their expedition had sought to avoid. Having no memory of anything to the contrary would be expedient as well for Hanna and Rocky, in the event that Dieter, or one of the demonic hordes even now rousing themselves to investigate this unexpected intrusion, decided to deep probe their minds for some alternative explanation for the unfortunate situation at hand. Both the Humvee and Dieter's vehicle were totally inoperable after their crushing collision, leaving their little party stranded in the expanse of shifting sands under a blazing full moon. Unfortunate, indeed, Antipas thought silently, a wan smile slowly creeping across his face as he watched a very animated fat beast struggle to extricate himself from the crumpled wreckage of his vehicle.

"Fucking shit!" Dieter announced, screaming at the top of his lungs, clearly not a happy camper. He lumbered over to the Humvee and peered into the mangled driver's compartment, taking in the remains of the driver strewn about the cabin. "You fucking piece of shit! I'm glad you're dead, you should never have been reanimated in the first place!" Sniffing the air, Dieter picked up the faint scent of the driver's soul, by now quite far away from the scene, and renewed his ranting. "Fucking dumb shit coward! Leaving us stranded in this fucking hellhole! I hope those demons tear your stinking piece-of-shit soul to fucking shreds for all eternity, you fucker!"

Hanna, regaining her sense of balance after the severe jostling from the crash, quickly picked up a more menacing presence swiftly heading in their direction.

"Incoming!" She shouted over Dieter's ranting. "Three, no five, five intruders closing fast...eleven o'clock...and they don't seem too friendly!"

"I hope you've got your cover story ready, Dieter," Rocky chimed in, as he began to pull his gear from the Humvee. He, for one, was always ready for any situation and he presently took out a small solid gold orb that Antipas recognized as being a particularly powerful pre-Sumerian talisman, perhaps Ubaidian in origin. From the brief glimpse that he got, Antipas knew it was in remarkably pristine condition considering its obvious antiquity…definitely a testament to its spiritual efficacy in warding off evil.

Dieter sniffed the air again and whatever scent it was he got hold of definitely sent a cold shiver through his august corpulence despite the searing heat. His eyes widened and sweat began profusely beading his brow only to drip down his thick jowls in steady rivulets. He began barking orders to his two subordinates, who set about in what Antipas viewed as a comic opera of great frenzied animation with very little actually being accomplished. He looked to the north northwest, where Hanna had first picked up the trace of movement. They would be there very soon, maybe five or six minutes at the most. The sweat began to pour off Dieter like a monsoon rain, soaking his clothes and making his every movement that much more labored. For all of his suave bluster during their meeting at the museum, in the face of the impending arrival of the demons from Ba'ir he was clearly afraid, Antipas noted, very afraid. Evidently, these were a class of demons with whom he was not used to dealing with, if he had encountered them at all before now, and it was obvious that Dieter wasn't too confident in his powers of persuasion with this bunch. Good, thought Antipas, it was the second favorable omen of the journey so far, the first, in a strange way, being the accident itself, which threw off all of Dieter's carefully laid plans and exposed him for the pompous lying bastard that he was.

"He'll not have an easy time talking his way out of what comes next," Antipas mused silently, his detached demeanor in stark contrast to the worry and concern of his compatriots.

When they had assembled at midnight in Amman at the museum, one of the crucial points they had hurriedly rushed over was the precise nature of their cover stories. Dieter had assured them that they would have a lot of time during the long drive across the desert to fine-tune their narratives and create a plausibly believable case in which all of their presences fit seamlessly together. Only they never did get around to nailing down that singularly crucial element. Like everything else so far on their excursion, it was one more screw up in Dieter's supposedly well-made Grand Plan. Antipas sent a quick mind pulse to both Hanna and Rocky on a frequency below Dieter's sensory threshold. He told them that in a tight situation where life hangs in the balance, the best policy is almost always the simplest…tell the truth. Since one of the reasons they were making this arduous journey into the wilderness was for the express purpose of securing a meeting with the Archangels Ornias or Berith, so that Antipas, the hero of Irian Jaya, could renew his allegiance to the cause of Ahriman, that was their best story. Hanna and Rocky were fellow travelers, personally recruited by Antipas, to help him usher in the Great Age of Ahriman on earth. Their unique gifts and privileged positions within PsyOps made them exceedingly valuable allies to have in the quest to strike the Sons of Light at their most vulnerable spot and render Heaven's defenses utterly impotent in the face of the Great Ahriman's overwhelming forces. That, he strongly argued, was the only story that would preserve their lives and guarantee them safe passage. What he didn't say was that Rocky had been more correct than he knew in his claim that Antipas' actions on the Carstensz Summit Ridge had made him a *very* important person in the demonic world. Even the despicable beasts of Ba'ir would know of his fame and thus be eager to be associated with his personage in whatever small way, if only just to give him accelerated passage through the Gate of ADAR. Hanna and Rocky quickly agreed and the three of them synchronized their psyches to be of one mind just as the incoming beasts of Ba'ir arrived in full battle gear.

There are few sights as terrifying than an Archon in his full ominous glory. For one thing, they're giants, standing a good five meters tall on average; and muscular beyond anything mere mortals can possibly conceive of. They prefer to wear nothing but the blood and entrails of their most recent victims and as a consequence they reek with the stench of death. Frequently they make necklaces from the severed heads of their enemies and proudly parade hearts and other body parts on the horns of their battle helmets. They are the shock troops of the Dark Lord, and known as much for their spectacular depravity in battle as for their fierce determination to exterminate anything that stands in their path. Archons are wont to kill first and ask questions later since they don't much care for such fine distinctions as living bodies or fresh souls. Thus, when they first appeared, casting huge dark shadows that obliterated the light of the moon, their first act was to gruesomely dispatch both of Dieter's accomplices, the same ones, Antipas noted, who had been with him during that fateful meeting at Hanna's museum, which now seemed a lifetime ago. The speed with which they attacked was surprising and when they were done, all that was left were two empty sacks of flesh, everything that had been enclosed in their bodies was strewn about the ground immediately surrounding Dieter. He stood alone in the middle of the carnage, shocked by what he must have perceived was to be his fate next. And it might certainly have been, had Antipas not interceded just as one of the Archons was readying to swing his double-sided axe in Dieter's direction.

"Spare him," Antipas called out in a surprisingly strong commanding voice that shocked Hanna and caused Rocky to raise an eyebrow. "He amuses me."

The Archon who was ready to strike paused, and looked squarely at the tall, thin reed of a man who dared to interrupt his sport. Before he could make another move, the leader of the group stepped forward, directly in front of Antipas, and peered down at him like some distasteful bug he was about to squash.

"That's close enough," Antipas barked in as deep a voice as he could manage. "I would hate to shed your noble blood unnecessarily, but if it comes to that I will without hesitation."

The giant Archon twisted his head quizzically as if not quite believing that such a miniscule excuse for manhood would possibly challenge him. He took another giant step toward Antipas. It was just the reaction that Antipas was hoping for and in a lightning quick move he jumped up and grabbed the big brute by the ears as he was twisting his head sideways. Antipas leveraged his full body weight to exaggerate the twisting of the big demon's head so severely that his neck snapped, dropping the humongous brute like a stone to the ground with a thud that caused the sand to ripple outward in big waves for a good ten meters in all directions.

As the remaining Archons swiftly reacted to the shocking death of their leader, Rocky produced the golden orb he had been holding behind his back.

"Ehyeh asher Ehyeh" he whispered, using one of the Seven Sacred Names to send a powerful spell over the Archons as they raised their weapons to attack.

"Antipas!" Hanna yelled out as one of the Archons brought his heavily spiked mace down on Antipas' head. She formed her thoughts into a huge spear of pure energy and hurtled it into the chest of the demon, where it burst into a massive fireball that totally engulfed the beast, sending him fleeing into the desert screaming as he burned to death, even as she feared the worse for her beloved Antipas. Another Archon swung his sword to decapitate Hanna in retaliation soon after she fired off her psychic dart.

But the effect of Rocky's magical spell was to make the Archons' weapons turn to dust as soon as they came into contact with their intended target, thus rendering them ineffectual. Hanna was knocked backward by the impact of the blow but was otherwise unharmed. Antipas too escaped unscathed, except for what felt like a huge bag of sand breaking over his head, which caused his glasses to become so thickly covered in dust and grit that he was momentarily blinded. He never saw the other three Archons striking at him but he certainly felt the impact of yet more sand and dirt being heaped upon him. In the heat and confusion of the sudden attack, it was almost lost on the three of them that Dieter had used the opportunity to scuttle away from the scene, no doubt trying to escape any possible harm falling in his direction, particularly given the swift execution of his two compatriots. But a very fat man moves exceedingly slowly across a shifting terrain of loose sand, especially when he's burdened trying to carry whatever thing of value that he most covets, which in Dieter's case was a heavy metal box filled with his most prized magical weaponry. One of the Archons quickly took note and hurled a heavy serrated throwing knife at Dieter, which struck him hard at the back of his neck. Had the blade not been affected by Rocky's spell, Dieter would have been holding his head in his hands, but as it was, he was flung face first into the ground from the force of the blow, sucking down a large quantity of sand in the process. He sat up, choking, cursing and spitting wildly, trying to get the sand out of his mouth and nose.

Meanwhile, Antipas, Hanna and Rocky moved closer together in a tactical position that allowed them to combine their psychic energy fields as they prepared themselves for yet another assault from the remaining Archons, who were clearly incensed that their weapons had been rendered useless. They threw down their spears and axes and instead seemed ready to use their bare hands to annihilate their surprisingly audacious and quick-witted foes. But something quite unexpected happened that forestalled any additional violence from the demons. Their next in command seemed to have heard Hanna yelling Antipas' name and just as his two comrades were set to rush the humans, the de facto leader grabbed the shoulders of his fellows and held them back.

"Wait!" he shouted to the two Archons and then pointed at Antipas. "The female called him 'Antipas,'" he intoned gravely.

"Lord Antipas?" one of the Archons repeated, his voice a mixture of confusion and awe.

"The same," said their leader. He stood ramrod straight and slowly approached the tight circle of Antipas and his colleagues. Remembering the fate of his former commander, whose body was plainly in view off to the side, the Archon stopped at a safe distance from Antipas before addressing him directly.

"You there," he thundered, his finger zapping the air, charging it and sending ripples of soft energy directly in Antipas' direction to let him know exactly to whom he was speaking. "In who's name do we have the honor of fighting?"

Immediately Hanna sent a thought wave to Antipas.

"Careful, Tip, it's a trick question," she signaled using their special frequency, with a newfound steeliness in her aura that he found positively sexy.

"I fight for Ahriman," Antipas replied evenly, showing no emotion in his voice.

"As do we," the Archon responded, with seeming approval. "But who is it that fights so fiercely and well on behalf of our Gracious Lord and Master?"

"I am he that Berith praised, beloved of Ornias, who is second only to the Dark Lord."

The Archon arched his large, heavy eyebrows and almost whispered his next question, clearly anticipating the reply.

"And what do they call you?"

"They call me Antipas Pergamos."

Now it was the demons' turn to huddle amongst themselves, clearly agitated by the revelation that they were facing off against a favorite of the Archangel Berith, their direct commander in chief. Antipas felt their intense probing of his mind and body seeking to verify what they had been told. He knew that they must have also probed Hanna and Rocky as well, since Hanna gasped audibly several times and shook herself vigorously at one point. After a few more minutes of heated gesticulations and the stomping of feet which made the ground reverberate, nearly knocking Antipas and his colleagues off balance, the lead Archon again addressed Antipas.

"We know Antipas Pergamos, beloved of Berith. Had you but made yourself known to us at the outset we would have prepared a more fitting greeting for one so esteemed. The sacrifice of only two of our number is totally inadequate for such an august presence. When we accompany you back to our base, we shall quickly make amends."

Rocky sent Antipas a short psychic message burst.

"Yes, had they known it was you they might have killed us all under the guise of honoring your august ass!" he quipped. "And don't let all that fancy talk swell your big head, either, I've still got a few more tricks up my sleeve."

Antipas smiled.

"Now, now Rocky, what on earth are you talking about?" he replied telepathically, even as he maintained eye contact with the lead Archon.

Addressing the Archon, Antipas demanded that no further attempts be made to harm any member of his party.

"You must be…hungry, Lord Antipas?" the Archon replied, clearly referencing the large crimson plume that arced above Antipas' head. "Perhaps you will at least take pleasure in the soul of that fat beast over yonder, who is of no consequence to either the living or the dead?"

The Archon pointed at Dieter, who quickly sprang to attention at the mere hint of his being sacrificed in order that Antipas could feast on his soul. Antipas gave Dieter a look of mock agreement, which served to put the fat man into a serious swoon, falling flat on his back.

"Yes, I am hungry," Antipas responded, "very hungry."

Immediately one of the Archons raced over and grabbed Dieter by the throat, lifting him clear off the ground in a single jerk. It was obvious that his next move would be to rip Dieter's head from his body so as to free his soul and present it to Antipas as a token of respect.

"But as agreeable as that idea sounds," Antipas interjected loudly, so that the Archon holding Dieter could hear him, "that fat beast owes me a great debt and his soul is my collateral. I want no harm to come to him while his debt is outstanding."

Even as he was held fast in the crushing grip of the Archon, fighting for every breath of air, Dieter pricked up his ears at Antipas' stunning announcement, which he knew would actually place him in a deeply more perilous situation since unbeknownst to Antipas his soul was already pledged to at least three other demons of great influence. The trade in souls is a matter of particular importance to the dark powers outside the everyday plain of existence. Transactions of such inordinately valuable substances are stringently regulated and very carefully documented so any hint of a contractual breech could have devastating consequences for the debtor…in this case, Dieter. To his way of thinking, instead of saving him, Antipas had just signed his death warrant, which put Dieter in an especially foul mood.

"That fucking half-breed can't be trusted worth a damn!" he fumed silently, making a mental note to keep his eye on Antipas from this point forward. As the Archon released his grip on him, Dieter fell back to earth, landing so hard on his ample rear end that he was completely knocked out of breath. He sat there for a long while, as he watched the Archons and the humans ready themselves for the trip back to Ba'ir. "Whatever else may be," he vowed to himself, "if I go down, I'm taking that fucking bastard with me!"

One of the Archons pulled a small package from a sack that hung over his shoulder, a sack Antipas noted that was made from human skin.

"Here, my Lord Antipas, we found this in the desert. Maybe it will suffice for the time being, until we get you back to our base, where there are considerably more delectable provisions for you to select from," the Archon intoned, as he handed Antipas the neat little bundle, tightly wrapped in what must have been the stomach lining of yet another poor victim from Ba'ir.

Antipas carefully opened the package and saw that it contained the disembodied soul of the driver, clearly prepared for consumption. Of course, thought Antipas, Archons also sustained themselves on the souls of the dead, except those of their own kind. He took particular note of the fact that for all of their newfound deference, the Archons most pointedly did not offer up the soul of one of their fallen brethren for him to satisfy his burning hunger with. That was both partly out of respect for their dead, as well as out of fear for what powers a Soul Eater might obtain by ingesting the soul of an Archon. It was well known that Soul Eaters incorporate into their being the particular strengths and wisdom of the souls they consume and over time they can become quite powerful entities, rivaling even an Archangel in their command of the dark arts. Perhaps, Antipas reasoned, they were just being cautious, in the event that Berith might desire to reanimate one of his special guards, which would also be a reasonable supposition, since the soul of an Archon can be revitalized ad infinitum. Regardless, he was starving and the driver's soul would do, for now.

They gathered up what gear they thought absolutely necessary and then stood in a circle, Antipas, Hanna, Rocky and Dieter, surrounded by the Archons. The trip back to Ba'ir would be considerably swifter than had they been driving in the old Humvees. The Archons enveloped themselves and their guests in a thick mist and they gently lifted off the ground and then began a slow acceleration which quickly gained speed until they were hurtling across the desert as fast as the soft light emitted by the moon fell through the heavens to land on the parched sand. Antipas felt something click into place inside his head, like a finely tuned movement slipping into gear. He smiled inwardly with satisfaction.

"Soon," he thought, "we shall know just what the devil you're made of Mr. Pergamos."

10 – HELL'S NINTH CIRCLE

"Oh my God!" Hanna gasped as they neared the dusty wreckage of what had once been the tidy little settlement of Ba'ir.

The first thing that hit them was the stench of death, which hung like a veil over every nook and cranny of the crumbling ruins that were all that remained of a sturdy desert town that had eked out a hard, seasonal living as goat herders, beside the banks of a somewhat ephemeral river that provided meager nourishment for the thin, parched soil following sporadic fits of torrential rain showers. The second thing that assaulted them were the bodies, or rather what was left of the bodies, strewn helter-skelter everywhere, like the sordid remnants of a mad flesh-eating zombie orgy that had gone on until every last living being had been butchered and heaped onto the banquet table.

"Steady there ol' girl," Rocky responded telepathically, trying to offer Hanna some sympathetic reassurance in his typically understated manner. "Don't let it overwhelm you. I'm quite sure there's worse yet to come."

As the Archons came to a stop in the center of the village square, Rocky's words almost seemed prophetic, for things did get worse…a lot worse…than anything the three humans could have ever imagined. Even Dieter, who regularly traveled in and out of some of the worst slime pits on either side of Hell, wasn't prepared for the sight that greeted them when they landed and immediately bent over, retching uncontrollably, which under the circumstances might have been by far the most rational response to the horrors the Archons had wrought in Ba'ir.

In the center of the square was a tower, standing maybe thirty-five feet high, that was composed of human bones – just the leg, thigh and arm bones – and formed into a vaguely triangular shape, about thirty meters around at the base, which narrowed to not more than three meters at the very top. Lashed to the sides of the tower, using garlands of disemboweled intestines as rope, were neat stacks of dismembered body parts – torsos arranged around the base and for the first several rows; then some rows of legs with feet attached, right legs on top of left legs, followed by rows of arms differentiated by right and left, then rows of heads, the faces contorted in grim witness to the unspeakable agony that must have preceded their final decapitation, near the top, crowned by mounds of the severed genitalia of both men and women. Vultures circled high overhead only to swoop down and pluck out an eye here or a tongue there or some other piece of flesh before flying off into the desert to consume their gruesome prize. Now it was Hanna's turn to console Rocky, as he turned away from the horrific scene, holding a hand to his mouth.

"Steady ol' boy," she offered calmly, with only a slight whisper of sarcasm in her voice. "It gets worse, you know."

For his part, Antipas was beyond any feelings of disgust, focusing his attention instead on the care and precision with which the Archons had gone about constructing their monument of death and wondering what motive might have prompted its creation. As he stared at the tower, the lead Archon seemed to have read his mind.

"This is to commemorate the momentous victory of our Great Lord over the Sons of Light!" he boasted proudly, as his comrades stomped their feet in approval, sending shock waves rippling outward through the sand. "Six-hundred fifty million infidels went to their graves this day!"

As the Archons shrieked and roared in celebration, their loud shouts roused more of their number to come out from their lairs amidst the ruins of the town. Soon the square was filled with a great celebration of Archons, some dancing around the tower while others fired off projectiles into the sky where their explosive tips caused huge fireballs that painted the whole scene with a macabre, reddish glow, not unlike the fires of Hell. Antipas surreptitiously surveyed their minds and pieced together the sad reason for their triumphant mood. Hanna and Rocky soon arrived at the same conclusion and together the three of them looked at each other with only the slightest glimmer of shock passing between them so as not to arouse the Archon's suspicions. Under the circumstances, it was actually a miracle that any of the remaining human inhabitants of Ba'ir were able to escape at all, for surely they too would have joined their brothers and sisters on the tower as part of the Archon's bacchanalia of grotesquerie. For that very day, all across planet Earth, in every major world capital and every major population center, a wave of spectacular explosions set off by a massive army of suicide bombers had erupted that killed at least six-hundred-fifty million people and left many tens of millions more maimed, missing or presumed dead. It was the most horrific loss of life on the planet in a single day since the Flood and the consequences were just as devastating. Widespread panic and fear gripped the human psyche en mass as the skies filled with a thick, black toxic sludge, like smoke from a funeral pyre. Indeed, it *was* a funeral pyre… for humankind and the world as they knew it. Many of the martyrs had come from places like Ba'ir and Irian Jaya where the Dark Forces. under the able direction of Berith, had infiltrated and turned remote, peaceful little enclaves into training grounds of seething hatred for everything that reeked of Heaven.

In a strange, twist of fate, Antipas noted dispassionately, their midnight trek across the Jordanian desert had actually saved them from the worst of the carnage, since Amman was no doubt among the capitals targeted…though judging by the tower in the square it was a debatable distinction as to which was worse – mass murder on a global scale or the more intimate, if still anonymous, wholesale murder of innocent villagers. Here at least, Antipas reasoned, with the full horror of what the Archons had wrought assaulting all of his senses, death was an infinitely more palpable reality. And as such, it was that much more unsettling to the psyche. It was no wonder then, he mused to himself as he watched Dieter, still retching, stagger to his knees and fall face first into the sand, that the Archons had opted to land at just this spot, in order to maximally shock and awe their unexpected visitors, hoping to throw them off balance, until they could determine exactly what to do with them.

And they nearly succeeded, certainly at least as far as Dieter was concerned. Hanna and Rocky, though, quickly got over their initial revulsion and were already actively trying to probe the rest of the village for any other survivors, albeit well under the radar of the impressively powerful Archons, whose own minds were busy as well, keeping a tight watch over the humans while heatedly debating their next moves. Only Antipas seemed to have remained above the fray, or so it seemed to him. As an exalted hero, the Archons pretty much left him alone, which gave him wide latitude to conduct his own subtle probing about the entire compound. He was looking for a very particular signature, one that he had become very familiar with during the long night at Esh Shaubak, so long ago now. And while there were traces of its having been present once, it was not then in actual residence. Still, it was the closest he had come to it since that fateful time.

"Patience, ol' boy," Antipas told himself, "patience. We'll meet again, just give it time."

He allowed himself only a fleeting flicker of hopefulness, which the Archons would have surely seize upon if they had detected it since "Hope" was the one human quality that drove demons into a mad rage, being the single emotion that they could no longer partake in after their fall from Grace. But Antipas was defiantly hopeful that soon his own particular mission, quite apart from anything that PsyOps, Rocky or Hanna had in mind, would come to its long awaited final conclusion.

"We should try to cajole them into taking us through the Gate as soon as possible," Rocky signaled telepathically, interrupting Antipas' quite reflections.

"Well done, Rocky," Antipas mused still deeper into his psyche, well beyond even Rocky's detection. He had used the exact same frequency that Hanna and Antipas had developed for their most private sharings. "You're a fast learner, you old dog."

This time, Antipas allowed himself to smile broadly as he turned to gaze directly at the good Major, who was puzzled by the gesture. As he suspected, his smile immediately drew the attention of the Archons.

"So, my Lord, you approve of our small tribute to the triumph of our Great Leader?" one of the Archons, a new one Antipas noted, who had joined the gathering in the square well after the others and who clearly possessed some authority over their ranks, called out to him.

As the Archon spoke, those in his way quickly and respectfully moved to one side so that he could walk unimpeded to stand in front of Antipas. He reached down a massive hand and stroked the top of Antipas' head. It was also a quite subtle show of force – Antipas felt an incredibly painful pinch of his scalp, as the Archon tugged at his thick red plume, causing a slight trickle of blood from where a small clump of his hair had been pulled out by the roots – no one watching would have been any the wiser, yet it conveyed its much darker truth in a way that was not lost on Antipas as his head, coddled in the palm of the giant Archon's hand, was forcibly guided to stare at the tower once more. There would be absolutely no tolerance for additional "heroics" on Antipas' part, the Archon suggestively signaled, his vaunted celebrity be damned. All Antipas could do, with his head still firmly gripped by his interlocutor, was nod in affirmation. Pleased that his message had been received, the Archon turned his attention next to Hanna.

"You have excellent tastes in women, my dear Antipas," the Archon said in a loud, booming, theatrical voice that made sure all those gathered in the square would hear him, as he flashed a salacious grin at Hanna. "It's been quite a while since I've indulged in such pleasures, but the mind still remembers their charms."

"And so does that twig between your legs!" one of the other Archons shouted out from the rear of the crowd, to the great amusement of the general assembly, who roared with ribald laughter.

As the Archons bantered back and forth with their supposed superior in increasingly suggestive tones, an undercurrent of aggressiveness began to fill the air with a palpable sense of latent violence, and it seemed to Hanna, Rocky and even Antipas that the situation could very easily get out of hand. The three humans took advantage of the Archons' preoccupation and stealthily repositioned themselves into a fighting posture, with Antipas and Rocky standing just in front of Hanna, to one side of the square, with the tower immediately behind them.

"Hey guys," Hanna signaled on their special frequency. "I'm not some helpless damsel in distress. I can take care of myself, okay?" she chided, more than a little miffed at being relegated to the rear. "After all, I took down one of those bastards too, remember?"

"Yeah, I remember," Antipas replied evenly. "But that was then, this is now. And right now there's a huge mob of increasingly angry giant demons arguing over whose monster dick can make you scream the loudest and frankly, I'm not keen on letting any of them find out the answer."

"Oh Tip, so you *do* care after all?" Hanna teased, trying to leaven the gravity of the situation.

"Listen you two," Rocky interrupted sharply, like a no nonsense Mother Superior keeping her charges in line, "can we stay focused on the matter at hand, here, please? There's something coming this way and judging by the energy vortex emanating from it, whatever it is, it's fucking huge."

As Hanna and Antipas got the first waves of the force field that Rocky had referred to, the three of them crouched together even more tightly in anticipation of a possible assault from the new entity that was heading directly for the square. They could all clearly feel the seething distaste for anything even remotely human that the entity so strongly projected and they ran mental checks of all the potential weapons readily at their disposal. Even Dieter was shocked out of his heaving stupor by the sharp scent of the approaching entity. He began to scratch frantically at the ground around him, trying to make a hole big enough for him to hide his corpulent ass in, but the sand in the square was so thoroughly saturated with dried blood that it was as hard as cement. Eventually even the Archons arguing in the square became aware of the approaching presence and they immediately fell into a hushed silence, like small children caught red-handed doing something they knew they shouldn't have by an angry parent, as they awaited the imminent arrival of the mysterious stranger.

Antipas carefully sifted through the complex layers of the stranger's signature for some clue as to who, or what, it might be, but he came up with nothing. That in itself told him that they were about to be in the presence of a very high-ranking demon, perhaps even a Prince of Hell, since the lack of any discernible markers in the astral signature of a being is only found among the most elite of the Fallen Angels. Given their proximity to the Gate of ADAR, Antipas reasoned, if it *was* a very important personage headed their way, then Ornias' High Command must be keenly aware of the presence of Antipas and company. The death of not one, but two, Archons in the space of only a few minutes would certainly have raised a huge alarm, since there are only two forces that can kill an Archon: Soul Eaters, of course, since there are no entities save Yahweh that are off limits for them; and... *ANGELS* above the rank of Seraphim! Antipas' eyes widened with a sudden realization that had surprisingly escaped his consciousness. He turned to look at his precious Hanna, defiantly balanced on the balls of her feet, that beautiful face taught with determination, ready for anything, a bright white plume waving proudly above her head. Antipas blinked again, trying to put the puzzle together before the entity arrived. The plume was definitely not the signifier of a high celestial being, yet there was no mistaking the fact that she took down an Archon with just a single thought.

"Curiouser and curiouser, Ms. Hanna al-Noori," Antipas mused silently, trying not to give any hint of the depth of his thoughts as he gazed admiringly at his beloved mistress.

His thoughts were quickly interrupted as a dark gust suddenly swirled into the middle of the square, kicking up a thick cloud of dust that forced the crowd of Archons slightly to one side as it coalesced into an ephemeral, vaguely humanoid sharp. The gust was accompanied by an awful wailing noise, like the sound of a million souls in torment, which was so loud as to be somewhat disorienting. Rocky, who was closest to the whirling mass, plucked a pair of earplugs from the pocket of his Tilley Excursion Vest and secured them firmly in place.

"Try not to focus on the sound," he signaled to Antipas and Hanna. "It's like the siren's call that lures sailors to their death."

Hanna had already surmised as much and Antipas noted that she had taken similar precautions. As a Soul Eater, Antipas had an innate immunity to this particular form of magic. Instead, he was more intrigued by how the entity chose to manifest itself and broadcast its presence. Soon, the swirling wisps of dark matter began to congeal into a fairly imposing specter, so large as to make the Archons look very small in comparison, completely clothed in a flowing black leather robe, edged by a thick crimson border that swirled like a river of blood rippling around its neck, sleeves and hem, and which radiated a metallic glow as if from some inner light. The Archons to a man knelt down onto one knee and bowed their heads in unison. This act of fealty observed, the entity completed its transformation into a being of impressive stature and great seriousness of bearing. His complexion was a dusky caramel and his hair a wooly mass of bright ginger dreadlocks that fell well past his narrow waist. His facial features were fine, almost precious in their delicateness. He was quite stunning to look at, beautiful even, with a vaguely effeminate quality which only slightly softened the severity of his demeanor. Antipas immediately thought of an iron fist in a velvet glove as an apt metaphor to describe the stranger. And as soon as his reconstitution was complete, he quickly showed that he was an entity not to be trifled with.

"Where are they?" the stranger demanded of the lead Archon, in a strong baritone voice that rumbled deep in the pit of Antipas' stomach.

"My Lord Marquis Andras," the Archon answered, his head still deeply bowed. "They are here, Your Lordship," he said, pointing to a sack that had been hurriedly passed to him from somewhere within the assembled masses behind him.

The Marquis pointed at the sack and it effortlessly flew from the Archon holding it to a position about waist high and some three feet away from him. There, after he cast a silent spell upon the sack, it opened and the two souls contained within it fell out onto the ground.

"Arise!" the Marquis snapped impatiently.

And arise they did, tentatively at first, but as they began to stand up, they again took on the same qualities that they had had in their previous life. Soon, two new, fully formed Archons stood proudly in front of their master. When they were totally reanimated, they knelt down and bowed their heads, just as their comrades had done. The Marquis immediately flew into a horrific rage, cursing the two Archons in an unfamiliar dialect that Antipas thought was vaguely similar to ancient Akkadian, and then hurled a massive fireball at the two which resulted in their complete annihilation. This time, there was nothing left of them to be reanimated. It was total, absolute, irrevocable destruction leaving only a small, smoke-filled depression in the sand where each of the Archons had previously stood. The fierceness of it and the suddenness with which he struck sent a noticeable chill through the ranks of the Archons.

"We will not tolerate weakness of any kind," the Marquis Andras shouted, the power of his voice throwing the first several rows of Archons off balance, forcing the rest to steady themselves with both hands as they knelt. "How *disgusting*! To be defeated by a *woman*, of all things!"

The way he spat out the word "woman" made plain his feelings about Hanna, but the Marquis never once looked directly at her, Antipas observed.

"Could it be that the Marquis knows who and what she is?" Antipas wondered to himself. "And how could he, her supposed lover, have been so blind for so long?" He vowed he would be much more observant from now on.

"You can put down your little trinkets, Rocky," the Marquis said wearily, as he turned to address the Major directly. "Don't insult our intelligence by thinking such stupid trifles have any power over us here. We are not amused. "

As the Marquis waved a dismissive hand in the Major's direction, it seemed as if all of the various magical instruments hidden in the multiple pockets of the Major's vest all melted and began to gush like so many fountains as they poured their contents into a giant metallic puddle at his feet.

"And as for you," the Marquis said, glaring menacingly at Antipas, "we have been expecting *you* for some time. In fact, we were beginning to wonder if you had gone soft on us after spending so much time in the presence of these, these..." he paused, searching for the right word, before smiling so chillingly that it felt as if the hot desert air suddenly turned to frost before he continued. "*Vermin*," the Marquis spat out at last, curling his lips so as to emphatically punctuate each vowel and syllable.

It was a lot of new information for Antipas to wrap his mind around, not the least of which was who, exactly, is this Great Marquis of Hell, Lord Andras, who seemed to know all about him but about whom he was completely clueless? As well, when and how had the Marquis and Rocky crossed paths? But most pressing to him, as he felt the temperature rising again with the waning of the moon as she prepared to give way to the Lord of the Daytime sky, was how he was going to protect his friends from what increasingly looked to be a bad situation getting still worse. It was clearly evident that Lord Andras was not above annihilating Hanna, Rocky and even Dieter without so much as batting an eye. The fact that they existed was provocation enough for him to unleash some hideously painful form of death. Antipas' mind raced through a myriad of scenarios and possibilities, trying to find some fulcrum with which to leverage a path forward that didn't end in disaster.

The Marquis looked Antipas square in the face, probing every atom of his being.

"Come," he scowled, clearly unhappy at not having found some scintilla of evidence to justify Antipas' immediate vaporization. "They're expecting us and we're already late."

As the sand began to swirl around his feet as the Marquis prepared to depart, Antipas decided that he had nothing to lose and he boldly addressed the Marquis.

"What about my colleagues?" he challenged. "I took great pains to bring them with me and they have valuable intelligence to share with the High Command."

The Marquis, clearly not accustomed to being addressed without his permission and with a total lack of the customary deference his position demanded, spun quickly around and grabbed

Antipas by the throat, lifting him completely off the ground, and held him mere inches from his face. His eyes flashed with a burning hatred that caused them to change color from a deep, chocolate brown to a bright, blood orange. If he were going to die, Antipas thought, this was the moment. But surprisingly, the Marquis suddenly flicked him to the ground and then turned to the Archons.

"Bring them," he commanded, in a voice so devoid of emotion that the air once again chilled by a good ten degrees.

The Archons immediately rushed to grab hold of Hanna, viciously groping and pawing at her body. Rocky did his best to keep between her and the chaotic legions, despite getting severely beaten about the head and shoulders by the angry mob. Dieter found himself surprisingly forgotten by the surging mob of Archons and began to quietly slink away from the fracas. He might have made a clean get-away if he hadn't tripped over the dismembered torso of an unfortunate villager that had not yet been added to the Tower. When he examined the remains more closely, he landed hard on his back and the force of his fall must have caused him considerable pain, since he inadvertently yelled out loudly enough to alert an Archon who quickly leapt over to rudely drag him back, slapping him every step of the way with the flat side of his razor-sharp kirpan. Well, that certainly explained the failure of Dieter's expected comrades to meet them as planned,

Antipas noted dryly. The poor bastard had just missed his chance to escape with the rest of the fleeing villagers.

"ALIVE!" the Marquis shouted as an afterthought, already half disappearing within a thick black cloud that also tightly wound around Antipas.

Soon, Antipas was being hurled through space, just behind the Marquis, heading toward the Gate of ADAR.

"Well, not quite the smooth entrance I had hoped to make, but it'll have to do," Antipas mused quietly as he observed the warm glow of the sun break over the crest of the mountains on the far eastern horizon. He knew that the Marquis would be too preoccupied with navigating their passage through the ethereal plane between the worlds to pay much attention to his psychic wanderings. But from Antipas' perspective, his plans were unfolding about as well as he could have expected. The fact that the demons had struck a massive blow against humanity wasn't yet a sign of his failure…more like the "shock" before the "awe" was unleashed. There was still time to change the path of lightening as it left its bottle. At least, he hoped.

"I can feel the fat lady warming up her pipes even now," he chuckled silently to himself, as he settled in to enjoy the ride back to the Gate and his appointment with destiny.

11 – SANCTUM SANCTORUM

Hanna was roused out of a deep stupor by a sharp pain in her right shoulder. As she regained more of her consciousness, she realized that her body was aflame with tender points of searing discomfort that intensified with her wakefulness. Her mind started to run through a checklist – Fingers? Very sensitive…but nothing broken; Arms? Left is okay…right one not so good; Torso? Sharp pains… right side and back… not good, but still serviceable she hoped; Thighs? Definitely bruised, especially on the right; Legs? Left feels okay, kind of…can't feel anything below the right knee…not good; Feet? Ditto…right one just doesn't register; Internal organs? Heart and lungs functioning normally…though deep breaths are difficult…maybe some rib damage?…doesn't feel broken…otherwise, everything else seems to be functioning okay;…Oh!...and *there*…some superficial tenderness only…no trauma…no penetration…thank God!...Rocky will be relieved about that; Oops!, hurts to smile…check that. Okay then, status report? It seems my right side is in a world of hurt…and I'm lying on my right side…hard floor…lumpy…sharp…rocks! Ouch! Okay…check…that explains it…mostly.

Hanna spent a good long while longer trying to fully remember everything that had happened since they left Ba'ir in the company of the Archons. It was a tough slog. Her head was just too clouded by a dense haze that she struggled to break free of…had she been drugged, she wondered? It would not have been out of the question, since Archons are known to put their intended victims into a drug-induced trance while they determined exactly what hideous form of torture would be cruelest to inflict on them. Obviously she had been separated from her colleagues for some reason…but whether that bode ill or not was still undetermined. Gradually, more and more of her faculties came back and she began to feel strong enough to attempt to move her body to ascertain the full extent of the injuries to her right leg.

"Hanna."

She stopped suddenly, startled by the voice softly murmuring at a deep level of her psyche. Hanna vaguely remembered that voice…but it had been a very long time ago when last she encountered it.

"Hanna, it's all right."

She couldn't believe that she was actually hearing it now…telepathically at least. How had *he* found her *here*?

"Hanna, your leg is badly broken from the fall but I will heal it for you now."

As soon as the voice spoke, Hanna felt a powerful, deep-tingling sensation all along her right side, followed by a wave of warmth that seemed to erupt from out of her very bones. The heat gradually increased, especially along that portion of her right leg that she could still feel, until it was searing hot, yet strangely soothing, releasing every trace of the various pains and traumas that had bedeviled her. It felt so good that she gradually slipped into a deep dreamlike state, her Third Eye opening wide, where at last she was able to remember everything. She remembered that Tip was considered a hero which conferred some status upon him, even though the distinctly ill-tempered Marquis didn't seem to be impressed by it. And didn't the Marquis also say "they" had been expecting him? She remembered the way the filthy Archons had fought over her, trying to get as close to her as possible as they lifted off the ground for the trip back to the Gate. She recalled the coarseness of their extraordinarily large fingers and hands roughly grabbing, touching, probing and feeling her body. Their collective stench was even worse than their crude pawing of her breasts. She felt relief at being able to breathe without getting nauseated. She remembered Rocky trying to protect her modesty and getting severely beaten for his trouble, poor brave fool. She hoped he was okay. She remembered being dragged down the dank corridor leading to her cell by her wrists, her feet flailing above the ground, and then being forcibly flung inside, where she crashed against a hard, stone wall, before bouncing backwards to the rock strewn floor, breaking her lower leg. Just thinking of Tip and Rocky helped to completely restore her psychic powers and she felt gratified that she could at last pick out their signatures amidst all the confusing background noise that began to explode from all around her. They were both alive and that was a good start, she reasoned.

"Hanna, they know who you are. They will be coming back soon and you mustn't be here when they return."

That voice again…and this time, she could clearly see its source. He hadn't changed in the least, despite the eternity of time which had passed since they were together last. But then, why should he? Time is a meaningless concept for spiritual beings. One hour, one day, one week, a millennium…what difference does it make to a demi-God? She was glad Aaron was here. Her spirit felt a sense of relief and comfort that he would be part of whatever that was to come. Of course, she was very well aware of his great valor at Esh Shaubak and before that at the Gate of ELUL, which in retrospect was the opening battle of the present conflict. He was a legend among the Elder Gods and they had come to rely on his fearlessness and daring in the fight against the Forces of Darkness. She had been part of the Angelic Order of Erelim when her revered leader, Tzaphkiel, the Archangel of Binah, incarnated her into human form, carefully disguising her soul as that of a lowly initiate bearing a bright white plume, and sent her upon the direct order of the Archangel Michael expressly to help Aaron in this most delicate Earthly mission, which the Elder Gods hoped would finally end the threat to Creation posed by the Ancient Ones once and for all. But instead, now Aaron was helping her. She felt frustrated by the frailties of the flesh which encased her. Erelim were supposed to be the Brave Ones, warriors renowned for their valor and courage in defending the Throne of Heaven against all enemies, not for being weak, helpless females who couldn't save themselves from danger.

"Sorry, Hanna, there will be time for rumination later. Now, we have to get you out of here. Take my hand."

Still deep in the trance of her Third Eye, Hanna saw the proffered hand of Aaron reaching out from the Anupadaka Plane and she grasped it with the hand of her Astral body. His incredible spiritual strength lifted her out of the pitch black dungeon into which she had been thrown by the Archons and into a liminal space infused with a brilliant white light.

"You'll be okay here for the moment," Aaron gently counseled.

"But what about you?" Hanna replied, relieved to be in a safe redoubt despite being in the belly of the Beast. "Shouldn't I be going with you?"

"Not yet, Hanna," Aaron responded, his voice trailing off as his spirit began to take leave. "He senses I am here, too, and it might be even more perilous for you if he learns of my mission before it's completed."

She didn't need to ask who it was that Aaron was referring to. Even as he spoke, she instantly saw a vision of Tip, sitting maybe a little too comfortably in the presence of the Marquis and Berith. The three of them looked like fast friends…or co-conspirators against the Sons of Light. Using a very deep register, she read Tip's psychic signature and realized that he had finally figured out her well-kept secret. The killing of the Archon had been the tell-tale giveaway, since only Angels of the First Sphere – Seraphim, Cherubim or Erelim – could accomplish such a feat, besides Soul Eaters, of course. Erelim were in rarified celestial company and subordinate only to the mightiest of the Elder Gods. She noted that the Marquis was quite worried about the presence of a warrior-class Angel in their midst, so close to the launching of their final conquest of mankind. For his part, Tip was reveling in the grand game, trying to convince his nervous host that it was a singular triumph for him to have made such a catch. She smiled.

"I gotta hand it to Tip," she thought, "the man does play fast and loose on a high wire without a net. If anyone could convince two senior Princes of Hell that they had an Angel of God on their side, it would be Antipas Pergamos."

Just then, a sudden flash of inspiration hit her as an image of a very dejected Dieter sprang to her mind's eye. She smiled again, this time suffusing the light around her with a warm pinkish glow of deep satisfaction.

"Well Mr. Pergamos, I'll see your bet, and raise you one!"

* * *

Rocky waited until the footsteps of the ill-tempered Archon who had been escorting him had retreated to a faint echo, far down the long corridor leading away from the fetid holding cell into which he had been thrown, before making his move. Now that the Forces of Darkness had made their preliminary strike on the world of the Righteous, it would only be a matter of hours, at best, before they launched their main advance, unleashing the Apocalypse and destroying everything that God and man had created on the face of the earth. It was the demonic version of Shock and Awe…they had succeeded in shocking mankind with over six-hundred-fifty million killed in the massive waves of terrorist attacks that circled the globe; now, they were planning to awe it with a scale of destruction that defied imagination. Not even Enoch and the hoary prophets of Revelations could have foreseen the kind of Hellfire that was to come. In the brief span from his arrival at the Gate to the long march to his little cell, Rocky had seen enough of the demonic forces engaged in their last-minute drills to know that mankind's last best hope rested on the shoulders of a frightfully small and greatly overmatched team whose members were scattered about in this dastardly underground labyrinth. There had to have been several million Archons, at least, all armed to the teeth and ready to pour forth from their bunker in murderous rage once they were given the command. If the same held true at the other twenty-two Gates that Satan's minions had breached, then mankind was in for a very ugly time of it indeed. With all the frantic hustle and bustle of activity, it also seemed to him that the demons were far too busy making their final preparations to bother dealing with unexpected prisoners for the moment. The first piece of good fortune, as far as Rocky was concerned, was the fact that the Archons merely roughed him up and then promptly discarded him into this fetid cell. He hoped that was also the fate of Hanna, and perhaps even that snake Dieter who, given the paucity of their odds, necessarily had to be lumped in with the White Hats at this late stage of the still unfolding drama. They had to have been similarly dealt with, Rocky reasoned with absolutely no way of knowing for certain. It was an intention of spirit that he hoped could be made true if he put enough effort into forming the thought.

"Get a move on, ole chap," Rocky mumbled beneath his breath as he extracted a linen pouch containing one very special magical instrument from the lumbar pocket of his Excursion Vest.

It alone had survived the withering effect of the Marquis' extraordinarily effective spell. Fortunately, it was also his most powerful weapon, a solid silver breastplate inlaid with twelve precious jewels set in gold and arranged in four rows of three stones, each stone engraved with the name of one of the Twelve Tribes of the Patriarch. The breastplate had two golden chains that were affixed to its four corners, one that went around his neck; the other that went around his chest, centering the breastplate directly over his heart. When used with the Seven Sacred Words of Power the breastplate was a formidable instrument of destruction in its own right. The beauty of the instrument, though, was its subtly…it could as easily blast an opening through solid rock as it could quietly vaporize the lock of a dingy cell somewhere in the bowels of Hell. Rocky considered for a moment whether or not the lock would be monitored. Not feeling any residual auras around it, he whispered his intentions and watched as thick streams of purple light emanated from each stone and coalesced into a powerful beam that shot from the breastplate toward the lock and in a flash, the cell door sprang open.

"That's the trick," Rocky thought to himself with a wry smile. "Now comes the easy bit!"

He merged his powerful psyche with the innate spirit encapsulated in the twelve stones to create a vortex that allowed him to pass undetected through the twisting passageways of the labyrinth, searching for signs of his compatriots. He was drawn to one remote corner of the complex where, behind a four-foot thick steel door, he found the very strong signature of Dieter. It wasn't his first choice, by a longshot, but then, he chided himself, "beggars' can't be choosers," and he focused his thoughts on allowing him to pass through the solid steel door. The breastplate opened just enough space within the molecular structure of the steel for his body's atoms to slip past them, reconstituting themselves on the other side as a solid corporeal mass again. As he materialized, he began to pick up another signature, closing in on the same space. This time, Rocky was all smiles since it could only have been Fortune's blessing that delivered Hanna into the chamber at that exact moment.

"We simply must stop meeting like this, my dear," Rocky offered cheerfully, as Hanna's ethereal form became solid again as well.

"But darling I thought you lived for such surprises," she rejoined, sounding relieved to have found a fellow warrior to wage the good fight with.

They both laughed out loud.

"Fucking shit!" Dieter squealed in a high-pitched voice bordering on panic. "This isn't some freaking reunion! Hell's about to explode and we're at goddam ground zero!"

Rocky and Hanna both looked at Dieter, shaking like a leaf in a stiff breeze, and laughed again.

"Well, I'm afraid the ole bugger is right about that," Rocky replied, turning suddenly serious.

"True. Before coming here I saw Tip meeting with Berith and the Marquis. They seemed like fast friends." Hanna responded, matching his tone.

"I hope that our man is still following the script, but frankly I'm not willing to leave all our eggs in that basket."

"I know what you mean. Aaron agrees too."

"Aaron? He's here?" Rocky asked, suddenly beaming as Hanna nodded her head affirmatively. "Well that changes everything. We just might pull this thing off, after all."

"We have no time for idle chit chat!" Dieter screamed aloud. "Don't you know that those damnable demons out there are about to storm the Gate?! We've got to..."

Rocky turned to Dieter and gave him a sharp look that silenced him in mid-tirade.

"Look here," Rocky said sternly. "You are the miserable piece of shit that supplied those 'damnable demons,' as you so aptly call them, with the very arsenal that they are going to use against us. For that alone I would be perfectly justified in blowing your sorry ass to Kingdom come."

Dieter's eyes widened at Rocky's accusation. He knew it was true, but that was also why PsyOps had reached out to him in the first place.

"You already knew that," Dieter responded coolly, trying to inflate his importance. "It's why we're all here now. I told you I would get you inside the Gate and I've more than fulfilled my part of the bargain. You were the clever creatures with the big plans for what to do once you got here. So now what more do you want from me? Am I supposed to save humanity's collective ass, too?"

"Hey!" Hanna interjected sharply before a visibly agitated Rocky could respond. "This is neither the time nor the place for settling this." She gave both of them a withering glance. "Rocky, you and Dieter head for the main arms depot. I want you to create a spectacular diversion. We need to buy a little time."

Rocky and Dieter both looked at Hanna with startled faces.

"And what about you?" Rocky asked, regaining his composure.

"I've got an idea," Hanna rejoined, her face furrowed in deep thought. "But it's still too sketchy to risk bringing you along."

"But you're outnumbered down here."

"Aren't we all?" Hanna replied, laughing easily. "Hurry, as someone said, we don't have much time. Besides, I've got my Guardian Angel watching over me."

Hanna was already beginning to dissolve as her words echoed in the dank chamber. Rocky and Dieter eyed each other warily.

"Do you have any idea where that arms depot might be?" Rocky asked, barely concealing his contempt for the sweltering black blob staring back at him.

"As it so happens, I do," Dieter said evenly, clearly as dissatisfied at the enforced détente as Rocky was. "But I don't have any magical powers like you or that angel bitch. You'll have to carry me to get where we're going."

Rocky shuddered at the thought of trying to carry the odiously corpulent Dieter anywhere, let alone drag his sorry ass through Hell. Admittedly, Dieter was as familiar with the passages of Hell as only a native denizen could be. More to the point, though, they didn't have time to spare for his fat butt to waddle up and down the infinite passageways of the labyrinth. Rocky narrowed his eyes and stared at Dieter with loathsome contempt.

"Come along," Rocky snapped, holding out his hand toward Dieter. "But I promise you, we better head directly to the depot or I'll personally feed your stinkin' carcass to Cerberus myself."

As Dieter's hot, oily, fleshy hand secured a good grip, Rocky silently directed his thoughts on the twelve stones and soon the two of them vanished into the ether.

* * *

Antipas was choking on the indescribably foul stench emanating from his two hosts, even as he smiled graciously and laughed heartily at Berith's frequent, lame attempts at off-color humor meant to cement some supposed bond between the three of them solely on account of the meat dangling between their legs. He had never liked such loutish talk, especially in male dominated spaces like gyms and locker rooms where the added homoerotic sub-current amped up the vulgarities expressed, and it was even more distasteful to him now, in the company of two stinking demons on the eve of their conquest of humankind who felt an irrepressible urge to curry his favor by demeaning all things human and most particularly female. He amused himself with the thought that his demonic horndog hosts were actually trying to signal their desire to have a no-holes-barred, ass-banging orgy with him, which was certainly what most male humans who engaged in such coded vulgarities really meant by them. He tried to picture Berith and the Marquis naked, which wasn't altogether too difficult to imagine given what little clothing they wore, barely concealing their stunning physiques…not to mention their ample endowments. As first among God's creations these Fallen Angels were definitely a comely lot, Antipas conceded with a silent chuckle. He felt his dick swell slightly as the fantasy began to take on a life of its own. But then another whiff of that infernal stench wafted deep into his nasal passages, quickly snuffing out any erotic charge and rudely slapping him back into the present moment.

"Careful Berith, you're arousing our guest," the Marquis salaciously whispered aloud, slowly jerking his hand in mock masturbation as he winked in Antipas' direction.

"Fuck our guest," Berith bellowed, "I'm arousing myself!" He stood up with a flourish and flung open his long flowing robe to expose an incredibly impressive erection. "In fact, fucking our guest sounds like a pretty damn fine way to work off some of this excess energy!" he laughed as he rudely stroked himself. "How about it, Antipas? I know you're no virgin when it comes to some serious fucking!"

Antipas felt a sudden tension grip his body. This was not an unexpected turn of events, but the sudden fact of the prospect was surprising nonetheless given the seriousness of the current situation. Surely, with a major war only moments away, Ornias' most trusted commanders had more important things to attend to than screwing their honored guest, Antipas mused while trying to formulate a response to defuse what now seemed almost more of a threat than an invitation.

"Come on Berith, we don't have time for this," the Marquis testily interjected to Antipas' great surprise. "It's nearly the thirteenth hour. I don't know about you but I've got a couple of divisions to inspect before we launch the offensive and last time I checked they were getting their butts kicked by some bitch. A bitch, incidentally who is running loose in our very midst, in case you had forgotten."

Antipas silently sighed with a mixture of new found admiration for the Marquis' dogged commitment to duty and relief at the prospect of being saved from what would most definitely have been an unpleasant interlude at best.

"Oh don't be such a prick, my dear Andras!" Berith hissed, not at all amused at having his sport interrupted. "For starters that 'bitch,' as you so crudely put it, is not running loose! Our angelic guest is in one of our tightest security cells and in due time will cease to be of any possible threat to either you or our great cause. And as for your precious 'attack,' Ornias himself told me that the festivities won't begin until our Great Lord Ahriman, who is presently resting comfortably in His chambers, personally takes to the field with the initial vanguard. So come on, let's have a little harmless fun with our honored guest before time spirals out of our control."

At that moment, there was a knock on the door to the salon and an Archon entered silently, carrying a large silver platter covered by an impressive gold dome.

"Ah!" Berith squealed, clapping his hands together and rubbing his palms in furious glee. "Lunch is served!"

The Archon placed the platter on a low table in between Berith and the Marquis and then lifted off the lid with a flourish. Fresh souls, still steaming with the residue of their recent hosts, were heaped to overflowing the sides of the platter and suddenly Antipas felt a ravenous hunger course through his body. Berith, now totally distracted from more prurient thoughts, scooped up two big handfuls of the slippery eel-like souls wriggling in fear from their impending demise and began greedily stuffing himself. The Marquis too, allowing himself a respite from his martial concerns, picked around the edges of the platter before selecting a couple of particularly choice specimens, fat with accumulated sins too numerous to list and obviously of an ecclesiastical nature. With his hosts completely self-absorbed in sating themselves, Antipas tried to make sense of the information which they had inadvertently divulged.

An interesting, if initially somewhat oblique, development made perfect sense once he saw the platter of human souls. Six-hundred-fifty million human deaths would create a lot of empty vessels which the invading demonic hordes could temporarily reanimate so as to be able to survive in the otherwise hostile earthly environment while they consummated their conquest. This gave him some idea as to the scale of what was in the offing and roughly the strength of the Forces of Darkness that would soon be pouring through the Gates. Naturally, another by-product of the sudden carnage unleashed in the initial terror attacks would be enough fresh souls to fortify the fighting spirit of the millions of Archons and demons preparing for battle. He helped himself to a couple of thick morsels quivering near the bottom of the platter that looked to have been former high-ranking members of the Roman Curia. Antipas smiled inwardly. "Waste not, want not," he concluded at last, well below the psychic threshold of either of his two hosts. He would need the added sustenance himself, since the plan beginning to take shape in his mind would necessitate a considerable amount of effort to successfully pull-off…and that last bit wasn't guaranteed in the least.

His hosts also confirmed that at least Hanna was still alive, if momentarily confined to a cell somewhere. He knew that she was way more powerful than Berith gave her credit for and that despite Berith's smug assurances, Hanna would no doubt prove to be even more dangerous than the Marquis' worst imagined fears. With Hanna on his side, the scales of Fate might just be tilted ever so slightly in his favor. He sensed that she was even then making her move and while he had no clear idea of just what she was doing, he felt certain that whatever it was would prove to be helpful to his own cause. At least the resulting fireworks would make for a spectacular show.

But by far the single most important revelation of his unwitting hosts was that Ahriman was alive! Despite the seemingly fatal wounds inflicted on him at Esh Shaubak, the Great Satan had not only survived but he was going to personally lead his forces into battle to avenge the attempt on his life. PsyOps would no doubt be quite distressed to know about this major wrinkle in their carefully constructed plans, Antipas wryly observed. Certainly it would severely damage the stock of Cambions in PsyOps eyes, since they still blamed him for the inconclusive outcome at Esh Shaubak. But Ahriman…alive. That was truly a game changer. Aaron would be quite pissed to know that his foolish sacrifice had been in vain. Aaron. Antipas felt a sudden flicker of cold air bristle the hairs on the nape of his neck and he instantly knew that his old nemesis was very definitely nearby. Now, how could he turn that fact to his advantage, Antipas mused. A fleeting image of Rocky and Dieter suddenly flashed across Antipas' psyche and he smiled broadly. "Well, well, maybe there is a God after all," he chuckled aloud to the quizzical glances of his hosts, who clearly weren't on to his frequency and thus at a loss to understand the real reason for his sudden cheerfulness.

"I think he likes them, Andras," Berith jovially chimed, poking the Marquis on the knee. "I forgot that I had ordered these special delicacies to be collected from Rome following the initial blitzkrieg. You know how corrupt all those Cardinals and Archbishops are! I couldn't think of any more well-marinated and ripe exemplars of absolute total dissolution than the Princes of the Holy Roman Church!"

"Well I must say you have certainly outdone yourself, Berith," the Marquis added, picking fat slivers of soul residue from between his teeth with the edge of a knife-sharp fingernail. "You always serve up the best meals I have ever had."

"Ah my dear Marquis, soon there will be even better to come!" Berith replied with a hearty laugh.

12 – LAST THINGS

"Is He awake?" Ornias anxiously asked the obsequious attendant carefully closing the huge gilded door to the chamber of the Great Prince of the Sons of Darkness, the Angra Mainyu, Rightful Heir to the One True God, Ahriman the Almighty.

"Yes, my Lord, but His Highness has just this minute commanded to be left alone so that He might pray for the valor of His soon to be victorious armies," the attendant answered in a solemn whisper, lowering his whole body in a deep bow of respect to Ornias, who as the second most powerful entity in the dominion of the Dark Legions was not one to be turned away lightly from any door, not even that of the Great Lord Ahriman.

Ornias scowled and the horrified attendant flinched, falling prostrate at his feet in expectation of some horrible punishment for having caused the mighty Archangel displeasure from the news he had just imparted. But no punishment ensued and Ornias merely spat out a string of foul invectives as he turned abruptly, the hard tips of his long, muscular wings slamming the poor distraught vassal hard against the closed doors of the chamber in his wake, and stormed down the corridor transfixed in deep thought, totally oblivious to the tumult that swirled around him along the winding corridors of the labyrinth as legions of fearsome Archons and elite brigades of demons from throughout the far flung empire of Hell hurried to their forward positions while trying desperately to avoid a certain death by even the slightest unintended contact with the impressive bulk of their burly and irascible Supreme Commander.

"Well then," he sighed after a long while, as he neared the entrance to his suite, "I'll just have to handle this myself."

The squadron of Archons guarding his door quickly snapped to attention and crisply saluted. Ornias, still consumed in his own meditations, barely acknowledged them as he swept into the imposing warren of rooms that were the de facto nerve center of the demonic underworld. He was immediately approached by a bevy of assistants bearing urgent messages from the various unit commands making their final requests before the order to commence the invasion was given. But he sharply waived his hand in response, sending them all scurrying back to their stations as he entered his private inner chamber. He was frankly just not in the mood to be interrupted at the moment, dealing as he was with a much more pressing issue. Ornias, foregoing his usual dalliances, even ordered his favorite *aide de camp*, a smooth, lithe, copper-colored youth with long legs, a high, firm ass and possessed with phenomenal 'talents' for soothing his frequently agitated psyche, to leave, and settled himself behind his impressively huge and intricately ornate desk, entirely composed of the bleached bones of those unfortunate enough to have fallen foul of his pleasure.

"Damn you, Aaron! Damn you! I should have destroyed you the first chance I had. Not even that pretty little angel of yours could have saved your fucking ass then. Damn!"

Ornias still bristled at the very thought of what had transpired soon after the battle at the Gate of ELUL, when Aaron, with the divine aide of the Elder Gods in the form of an incarnated Seraphim angel, had barely thwarted Ornias' exploratory raid through one of the first Gates Between the Worlds that his forces had successfully breeched. Ornias had been trapped in the human plane of existence and, despite taking possession of a number of willing hosts deeply steeped in the occult practices of Black Magick, he found his immense powers severely constricted by the flesh and bone of ordinary mortals. Aaron, reeling from the loss of his beloved angel, Khydyra, had chased Ornias relentlessly over many eons as Ornias tried to make his way to another Gate through which to regain access to the domains of the Underworld. Once, early in their game of cat-and-mouse, Ornias had managed to turn the tables on Aaron and trap him. But because of the heavily charged atmosphere of the earthly realms and the dampening density of human flesh, Ornias could not finish off his opponent as he would have liked. Instead, all he could manage to accomplish was temporal damage to Aaron's earthly body, which, because he was an immortal Soul Eater, only resulted in a badly wounded Aaron slinking off to the Anupadaka Plane to regenerate himself and become an even more formidable opponent to deal with.

Ornias, who eventually succeeded in making his way back to the dark realms, was beside himself with rage at not having been able to eradicate Aaron there and then. And now, Aaron was back…and lurking somewhere within the very walls of his own Command Headquarters…just on the eve of the Great Lord Ahriman's final conquest over that pitiable pile of excrement known as *"Humanity."*

"Damn!" Ornias bellowed once more, his mellifluous, rumbling, baritone voice causing the solid rock walls to shudder as a network of fine superficial cracks erupted across their surface. "I don't care what the fucking hell you are now, you miserable jinn, nothing….NOTHING! will stop our Great Lord from assuming His rightful throne! Do you hear me! The pact was made upon His departure from Behesht…a thousand years, your pitiable Elder Gods said, a thousand years and our beloved Aiwas would be loosed again to reign over all Creation! Well it's *His* time now, damn it! It's HIS *TIME*!"

Ornias slammed his fist hard on the top of the desk as he ranted, driving the sharpened tips of its finely interwoven legs into the polished stone floor. Flecks of dust and rock flew up from the resultant depressions and started to coalesce into a swirling slurry of thick black smoke in the middle of the room. Ornias stood up from behind his desk and intoned a long, complex magical formula while slowly masturbating to a powerful orgasm. A thick white stream of his seed ejaculated into the center of the seething torrent, which immediately began congealing into a corporeal sludge that gradually took on a vaguely hominid form. Ornias closed his eyes and crystalized his most wicked thoughts into a sinuous ribbon of light that flowed from his Third Eye into the Sahasrara chakra of the partially formed hominid, a tulpa, animating it and giving it a solidly defined musculature. When he opened his eyes, Ornias grunted in approval at the stunningly beautiful androgynous creature that returned his gaze with stoic reserve.

"You are my mind made manifest," Ornias thundered at the tulpa. "Go now! Do not return to me until Aaron has been destroyed."

The tulpa, standing not more than five feet tall, with creamy chocolate-brown skin, jet-black braids of hair that fell to its broad shoulders, large, pale-grey eyes that flittered about the room observing everything in minute detail with a chilling, cold-blooded meanness, extremely agile and swift in its movements, turned away from its master without the slightest acknowledgment and disappeared into the ether, gifted with the most potent magick that Ornias possessed and single-mindedly focused on its assigned task. Satisfied, Ornias turned his attention back to the pressing details of the impending invasion and summoned his anxiously awaiting subordinates to his chambers, none of whom could fathom the meaning behind the broad impish smile that lit up his face as they entered, particularly since his conjugal slave was still outside.

Just as the staff arranged themselves in a semi-circle in front of Ornias' desk, the ground under their feet rippled violently, throwing them all to the floor in a great mass of confusion as urgent papers and thick notebooks flew in every direction as they fell. Ornias himself was tossed off of his throne and forced to dodge massive sections of the coffered ceiling as it crashed down, pinning some of his minions beneath its colossal weight. The outer chamber erupted in a cacophony of agonizing screams and panicked shouts as desperate demons and Archons struggled to free their injured comrades from under the avalanche of heavy debris that suddenly engulfed the Command Center. Pulverizing boulders as large as his own gargantuan frame with bolts of lightning, Ornias quickly made his way to the outer office only to see his once stately sanctuary transformed into a wasteland of rubble and carnage. Ornias immediately recognized the limp form of his beloved *aide de camp* lying face down just a few paces away from the potential safety of a narrow refuge, his body crushed under a massive pile of stone pillars that had fallen like dominoes from the mysterious explosion. With nothing left to support its massive weight, the great vaulted ceiling had partially collapsed as well, leaving the outer chamber buried in a wreckage of stone almost six meters deep. Ornias projected his psyche through the thick haze of dust thrown up by the cave-in to see that he would have to blast his way through the debris to even exit his chambers. Using his mind's eye, he also took inventory of how the rest of the gargantuan complex had fared and what he saw sent him into a blind rage.

Ornias let loose a furious blast of thunderbolts that quickly sliced through the heavy stone, literally melting a path before him, as he rushed across the vestibule to the doorway that led to the exterior corridor. As he reached the relative calm of the passageway, he was met by Berith and the Marquis Andras, both covered in a heavy layer of dust and smeared with blood from numerous gashes to their arms and torsos.

"What the fuck happened?" Berith screamed as soon as he saw the familiar form of his great friend materialize out of the haze.

"Aaron is here," Ornias replied through clenched teeth. "He thinks he can disrupt our plans but he has another thing coming!"

"He had to have had some divine help!" the Marquis quipped sharply, expressing his keen displeasure at the sudden turn of events. "That Angel bitch has a hand in this, no doubt!"

"Oh shut up, Andras!" Berith sneered. "I swear you must have a hard bone for her ass something bad..."

Ornias interrupted with a swift wave of his hand in front of Berith's face before he could continue. Ornias was well aware of the "angel bitch" to which Andras referred. He closed his eyes and entered a deep trance while Berith and Andras looked on. His facile mind easily slipped behind the veil of ordinary consciousness and began to systematically sift through the chaotic tumult of energy signatures swirling throughout the great labyrinthine caverns of the Command Center seeking unusual anomalies. In and among the multitudinous signatures of demons, Archons and various Princes of Hell, Ornias felt the echoes of several faint trace imprints quite different from the norm. He felt the karmic signature of Andras' 'angel bitch' moving rapidly through the warren of chambers, her being an Erelim of Celestial origin was marked by a very subtle distinction in her aura as opposed to that of the more exalted classes of Princes. It zigged and zagged seemingly at random as if attempting to hide its intended objective, but triangulating through her pattern of movement, Ornias intuited a strong hunch about where she was headed.

Two more signatures lingered not far from the epicenter of the explosion, which was at the main arms depot located four levels below that of the Central Command, a fact that in itself proved somewhat fortuitous since the primary force of the blast was contained by the sheer density of the subterranean rock, and could have been far more devastating had it been even one level higher. They were also on the move, but at a far slower pace than the Erelim, and seemingly headed on a vector that would intercept with her. One of those signatures seemed to be demonic in origin, though of a decidedly low caste, which was worrisome enough given the large contingent of minor demons mustered to headquarters for use in the initial onslaught through the Gate and into the Human realm, a particularly dangerous foray for denizens of the Dark Realms due to the hostile atmosphere found on the surface of Earth. The minor demons were mostly expendable in the main, given their absence of any special power or capability other than the brute force represented by their sheer numbers, and consequently of little importance. However there was one signature that raised far more serious cause for concern since its origin was harder to decipher. This signature was exceedingly complex and considerably more difficult to read, even for a magus of his exalted rank, and that gave Ornias a chilling pause. Could there be traitorous internal forces at work he wondered? Ornias shook his large, angular head abruptly, as the ringlet of short, Auburn dreadlocks crowning his otherwise bald head clung tightly to the edges of his darkly handsome face, and shrugged the broad naked expanse of his muscular shoulders, raising the full length of his flowing white wings completely off the polished stone floor, as Berith and the Marquis expectantly eyed the great Archangel as he towered over them.

"Well? Anything?" Berith asked anxiously.

"Our Great Leader has the situation under control," Ornias replied evenly, with just the slightest flicker of a smile hurriedly fleeting across his thick, full lips.

Both Berith and the Marquis nodded in unison, seemingly satisfied with his affirmation.

"Get to your posts. The moment we have long labored for is soon upon us and we shouldn't be left holding our dicks in some dank corridor while transcendent glory awaits!" Ornias cajoled, his powerful hands gently, but firmly, patting his compatriots on their backs while pushing them to leave. As his fellow Archangel and the Marquis disappeared down the corridor, sidestepping fallen beams and other wreckage from the blast, Ornias turned quickly in the opposite direction, clearing the way with intense waves of pure energy that emanated from the palm of his hand in great pulses of blinding crystal-blue light.

"I just hope I'm not too late for the party," he contemptuously whispered beneath his breath as he flew down the freshly opened passageway.

Ornias had not wanted to share with his companions just how extensive the damage had been as a result of the blast, mainly out of a concern to not distract them from the far more important and delicate operation that was just about ready to begin. Berith, his brother angel, was Ornias' most trusted second-in-command and exceptionally skilled in directing complex military engagements in the earthly realms based on his first-hand experiences during the Irian Jaya affair. At this late hour, the mission could ill afford to have the easily distracted Berith's attentions diverted. And the Marquis Andras, a true master executioner of the first rank, whose proven propensity for brutal depravity would be critical to the success of the opening salvos of the invasion, was absolutely needed at his position in the lead vanguards. If they had known all of what Ornias had seen, they would certainly have wanted to exact the cruelest revenge on the perpetrators of the craven plot and Ornias definitely did not need that complication.

In his quick psychic inventory, Ornias noted that half of the primary arms depot had been destroyed and several million crack Archon troops killed, either directly from the blast itself or as a result of the numerous cave-ins that had followed in its wake. Those potentially devastating losses on the eve of the campaign were somewhat tempered by the fact that, given the multilevel design of the underground bunker complex and the sturdiness of the rock out of which it was carved, there was still considerable fire power and many tens of millions more troops left totally unaffected in the main strike units stationed in their forward bunkers. And besides, Ornias consoled himself as he sped through a maze of blocked corridors and collapsed passageways, many of which were already starting to repair themselves, the Great Lord Ahriman's potent magick was hard at work throughout the damaged complex, making critical structural repairs and resurrecting multitudes of the fallen combatants for their upcoming role in the initial surge through the main Gate. Even, Ornias noted with particular delight as he silently gave thanks to the Almighty Dark Lord, his poor, young *aide de camp* would soon be able to provide his irreplaceable pleasures once again in due course. At best, Aaron and his accomplices had only succeeded in delaying by no more than a few moments the hellfire that was poised to be unleashed at the personal command of the Angra Mainyu himself. A command that was due to be given from the Great Hall of Gehinnam, a gargantuan underground basilica carved out of the living rock adjacent to the Gate of ADAR and built on top of the very sepulcher, now consecrated as the Grotto of La Clementina, where the cowardly assassination attempt on Ahriman's life had been made so many eons ago, and toward which Ornias was now headed with all the speed his own potent magick could muster.

"You're so predictable, Aaron," Ornias muttered aloud, as he flew up a curved staircase leading to the entrance to the Hall. "Really? Did you think I would fall for that stupid diversion? I know where you and your impudent rabble are going and trust me, you won't like what you find when you get there."

At the end of a long ceremonial corridor, opening onto a portico bedecked in highly polished stone and inlaid with the skeletons of the most wicked and infamous malefactors of human progress – Gautama Bhudda, Ashoka the Great, Jesus of Nazareth, Paul of Tarsus and Ahmad the Paraclete, among only the most notable – encased beneath clear slabs of pure crystal where they would be trod under the feet of Hell's most high and mighty for all eternity, Ornias slid open the ancient bronze Filarete Door leading to the vaulted nave of the basilica. Crossing a great disc of red porphyry stone standing out against the marble paving where the Princes of Hell are consecrated, his bare footsteps echoing in the still, cool air, Ornias quickly surveyed the Great Hall for any ethereal signatures and found that he was alone for the moment. He could feel the distinct ripples of energy preceding from the aura of the Great Ahriman and knew that His Eminence would soon enter La Clementina, the sacred prayer grotto just a few steps beneath the basilica's main High Altar of Callixtus, from where He would make the exalted pronouncement that would usher in His reign over Creation. Ornias probed deeper still and found the tell-tale markings of his tulpa, stealthily hunting for its prey in the Anupadaka Plane. He smiled. Cloaking his own powerful signature in a heavy essence of lapis lazuli to make himself completely invisible, Ornias diligently set about planting a diabolical trap for his expected visitors. Satisfied that his infernal preparations were complete at last, Ornias then spread his great wings and flew up to the Loggia of Longinus, carved into one of the four gigantic piers supporting the dome directly above the High Altar to covertly watch his plan unfold.

Hanna was the first to arrive. She immediately recognized the layout of the Great Hall, mirroring as it did the Throne of Heaven, which made perfect sense given that Ahriman was among the first of the Elder Gods' creations and thus was thoroughly familiar with the intimate architecture of Araboth, the seventh and highest of the Heavenly Realms. Previous angelic messengers had even passed on the sacred dimensions to the human race and it was copied many times over the aeons, most notably in Rome at St. Peter's Basilica. She instantly looked up at the four huge piers and the colonnaded niches carved into them searching for any signs of ambush but could feel nothing. Waving her palms in the sign of the cross, Hanna methodically traced the purifying symbol in all four directions, hoping that by so doing her magick could counteract any lingering evil lurking about the huge vaulted nave, its transepts and numerous chapels. When she was done, Hanna's Third Eye began to systematically survey the great nave in an effort to find the safest vantage point from which to launch a desperate last attempt at halting the demonic master plan.

"Funny, but I was just thinking of the same thing!" a familiar voice called from behind her. Hanna quickly turned and was relieved to see Rocky standing just in front of the High Altar as Dieter rushed down the steps leading to the Confessio searching for some sanctuary in which to hide his impossibly large girth from what he assumed would be the final suicidal battle that would prove the success or failure of their maniacal mission to avert Armageddon on earth.

"Good to see a friendly face," Hanna smiled as she walked towards Rocky. "Your little diversion was quite the blast! I'm sure it will take them awhile to repair the damage. That might buy us just the time we need."

"Yeah, well, I had a little help," Rocky replied, running his fingers along the edges of his bejeweled breastplate. Turning more serious, Rocky lowered his voice to a whisper. "Any signs of *them* yet?"

"Not yet," Hanna replied, her voice suddenly tense. "I've run a psychic scan and I can't even find lingering traces of them. Which seems more than a little strange to me. This is obviously the most important space in the whole complex and it should be swimming in demonic energy, especially that of the most high-ranking Archangels and Princes of Hell at the very least. Certainly if Ahriman were alive his energy signature would very much be present since I'm sure he would have used the High Altar on a regular, if not daily, basis. But there's just nothing at all."

"That is a bit odd," Rocky concurred while following Hanna's eyes as she continued to look about the richly coffered ceiling and intricately carved niches of the nave, many nearly impossible to make out, hidden as they were in deep shadows. "And what about our friend? Any sign of *him* yet?"

"You mean Antipas?" Hanna blurted out a bit too earnestly. "No, nothing, not a whiff of his signature," she continued, trying to be as neutral as possible but fearful that Rocky would nonetheless notice her deeply passionate concern for Tip's well-being.

"Well, then, if this is the right place, then we had better continue your efforts at locating a suitable defensive position. On first look, I can't say that I like anything here," Rocky said, his voice assuming the dispassionate staccato of the seasoned military commando, as his eyes shifted uneasily about the vast vaulted nave. "Everything is far, far too exposed for my comfort."

From the nether regions of the Confessio, which was a large cutout in the main floor of the nave and reached by a flight of seven steps (one for each of the Deadly Sins) descending into a small grotto where various niches had been carved out of the solid marble slabs which comprised it, a loud piercing scream erupted, filling the whole of the basilica with a horrific sound that reverberated endlessly throughout the deep vaults high up in the gilded domes over the central nave and transepts. Hanna and Rocky looked at each other in momentary confusion, before rushing down the semi-helical curve of marble steps to see what trouble Dieter had gotten himself into. When they reached the bottom of the steps, they were shocked to see a river of blood flowing from a shallow niche cut into the far wall directly in front of them. As their eyes followed the crimson trail back to the niche, Hanna was nearly overcome by the terrible sight which greeted them. Dieter, nailed upside down to an inverted silver cross and howling madly in excruciating pain, had been flayed alive, the entirety of his wretched black skin completely stripped from his bloated body, leaving a quivering pink mass of flesh bleeding profusely from his toes down to his head. Pinned to the front of the niche and hanging below his wailing body was the remnant of what had once been his most obvious mark of distinction – his dark, smooth, blacker-than-midnight hide – stretched taut as if it were an ornamental rug. There were no signs of any Archons or demons anywhere to be found and yet it was immediately obvious to Hanna and Rocky that they were not alone…and they were in mortal danger beyond their worst fears.

"It's a trap!" Rocky shouted, grabbing Hanna by the shoulder and turning to rush back up the stairs.

As his foot hit the first step, a huge spear of molten adamantite slammed into his back, knocking his body forward completely off its feet, before pinning him fast to the marble staircase.

"ROCKY!" Hanna screamed, just as the spear flew past her ear at lightening speed a split second before striking the Major with a brutal thwack.

As she dashed to reach him, though only a mere foot away, Hanna suddenly found herself in a withering barrage of flaming arrows that lit up the whole basilica with their phosphorescence. As quickly as she fended off one onslaught, another would begin raining down on her position. From what she could see briefly between the furious waves of her hands as she tried to repel the incoming projectiles before they could strike her or the injured

Rocky, it looked as if the arrows were originating from recesses in the corners high up on the ornate Baldacchino that towered over the High Altar and the opening of the Confessio, effectively enclosing it in a sacred power nexus. By entering into the Confessio, Hanna reasoned, Dieter had unwittingly broken through the plane of the nexus, thus causing its self-defense mechanisms to activate in order to repel the intruders. She now realized that her own attempt to spiritually cleanse the space had in fact merely intensified the power of the original nexus, making the barrage of hellfire even stronger. To make matters worse, the arrows had been tipped with Bane, a magical element that tunes itself to the signature of its target in order to enhance its destructive effect.

This being the very heart and soul of the Demonic Realm, the fury of the barrage of hellfire spewing down on them was unimaginable in its ferocity. Hanna noted that while Rocky was obviously in great distress, the spear had not delivered a fatal wound. She sensed that it too had been tipped with Bane and its purpose perhaps was simply that, to only incapacitate it victim, maybe in anticipation of some more nefarious injury to be inflicted later. Showing great pluck, Rocky made feeble attempts to pull the wicked spear out of the step to free up his range of motion, since it appeared that the breastplate was inaccessible while he was pinned. He must have realized the spear's intended purpose and wanted to extract himself before its mission could be completed. She desperately wanted to help him. However the constant onslaught of arrows were beginning to take a toll on Hanna, several had already pierced her skin, causing agonizing flesh wounds, the pain from which was starting to sap the speed with which she could respond to the next barrage.

She had to get Rocky and herself to a safe place, but where? If they retreated deeper into the Confessio, they risked even more terrifying attacks from the nexus as it defended itself. Yet if they tried to rush back to the main nave, they would be totally exposed, just as Rocky had feared, to any number of other potential assaults from forces that were most probably hidden in the nave and waiting for prime targets to attack. Moreover, if she even for an instant tried to help Rocky pull the spear from its deep seat in the step, countless deadly arrows would be certain to hit them both with potentially devastating consequences. She just had to find the strength to keep fending off the relentless barrage.

"Hanna!" the familiar voice once more called to her, "Run for the corridor behind you! I'll help Rocky!"

Hanna was overcome with relief and instantly started to run for the nearby corridor, which led into the complex of grottos beneath the main floor of the Great Hall. Out of the corner of her eye she saw Aaron's luminescent form beginning to materialize out of the Anupadaka Plane, his fiery glow creating a welcome shield from the steady barrage of arrows, and completely extract the spear that had pinned Rocky to the marble stairs. As the two of them began to make their way towards her, Hanna saw something else materialize out of the enigmatic ether. Before she could blink, the mysterious form suddenly attacked Aaron with a horrific volley of powerful thunderbolts that flew through his still nascent body, causing massive wounds just as he was most vulnerable. Aaron staggered from the surprise ambush but still kept hold of Rocky as he tried to get them both to the safety of the corridor. Hanna turned quickly and began firing lightening bolts point blank at the now fully materialized assailant, but her energy projectiles merely passed through the entity without any visible effects. The relentless barrage of arrows continued to rain down on the three of them and as Aaron's glow began to flicker worrisomely, more of them began to find their targets through the gaps in his's aura.

They were in a dreadful situation and Hanna now found herself having to save Aaron as well as Rocky. Rushing to the niche were Dieter was crucified, she desperately plucked his still howling body from the silver cross and hurtled him above her head, using his huge bulk as a shield from the barrage of arrows. She could feel any number of arrows striking his bulbous mass of flesh as she rushed back to her comrades. Perhaps, she reasoned, death would come quicker for him and end his suffering this way. Besides, of everything that she had tried, this was proving to be extremely effective at protecting her as she grabbed Aaron and Rocky and pulled them under Dieter's heavy body, enabling her to concentrate her psychic energy to neutralize the projectiles coming from the tulpa at their rear. Nearing the relative safety of the corridor, Hanna flung the almost lifeless form of Dieter high into the air behind them, where it attracted an especially punishing phalanx of arrows that reduced it to a smoldering pile of burnt meat. Meanwhile, Hanna was finally able to defeat the tulpa by sending one mighty surge directly from her Anahata chakra into the tulpa's Third Eye, vaporizing the evil thought form in a cloud of divine light. Hanna slumped to her knees in the corridor as Aaron and Rocky collapsed to the floor beside her. For the moment at least, they had found a refuge...no more arrows rained down on them and no diabolical tulpas pursued them.

Exhausted, Hanna reached over to Aaron's slumped body resting head down in a fetal position against the wall of the corridor, hoping against hope that he was still alive. But before she could get to him a large menacing shadow appeared on the floor before her, plunging the corridor into total darkness. She immediately looked up and the face she saw filled her with utter shock, followed by a fearsome dread.

"He was supposed to be DEAD!" Hanna screamed silently on her deepest most channel, causing Rocky to stir ever so slightly and crane his neck toward her before looking up at the shadow looming over them. "But here he is... *alive!*"

She bowed her head in complete and utter defeat as Rocky groaned and sunk into a deep slouch, his hand squeezed tight over his wound to staunch the bleeding, his mighty breastplate ripped apart by the spear as it exited his chest. This was it then. They had unquestionably failed in their mission to stop the Forces of Darkness from wreaking havoc upon Creation. Standing in front of them was everything that they had fought so desperately against. Majestically draped in a splendid purple robe fringed in gold brocade in the Sign of the Cross covering his modesty, the Great Prince of the Sons of Darkness, the Angra Mainyu, Rightful Heir to the One True God, Ahriman the Almighty, in His full glory, stared down at the whole sorry scene and began to laugh heartily.

"Bravo! Ornias, my son! Bravo!" Ahriman chuckled, his incredibly deep basso profondo voice rumbling throughout the whole of the nave. "At last, the moment we have been waiting so long for has arrived. And what special joy it is to celebrate our triumph with the capture of this odious vermin!"

"It was the least that I could do, Your Highness," Ornias replied, as he flew down from his secret hiding place up in the loggia and deferentially landed a few paces away from the Great Lord. "Especially seeing how *that* miserable piece of shit," Ornias continued with an elaborate wave of his hand which ruffled Dieter's smoking remains and sent pieces of them blowing about the polished marble floor like so many marbles scattering about, "tried to cheat Your Lordship out of that which was Your proper due by daring to sell his soul twice. And *this* filthy maggot," Ornias continued, giving Aaron's motionless body a vicious kick to the head for added emphasis, "had the galling audacity to attack Your Highness lo those many years ago not far from this very spot!"

"Now, now, my son," Ahriman mockingly pleaded. "Let us save what's left of him for the Dark Mass at Saint Peter's after our armies have taken Rome. I'm sure he'll make great sport for our honored Princes," he chortled, looking at the small cadre of honored nobles just entering the Confessio, who clapped approvingly in response. "And besides," Ahriman continued, "it will be such an auspicious way for his sojourn amongst our new Celestial Realms to come to its final conclusion."

Ornias and Ahriman shared a hearty laugh as they were joined by the Great Lord's personal army of Imperial Guards and a huge retinue of noblemen, priests and retainers. These last grabbed Rocky, still somewhat in shock from the wound inflicted by the spear, and Aaron, whose body had suffered some obviously serious wounds from Ornias' tulpa, and carried them up the marble steps to the main floor of the Great Hall. Another retainer scooped up the last of Dieter's remains and dumped them into a small satchel which he carried about his neck before following his comrades. Hanna, exhausted beyond measure by her earlier exertions, could only shake her head in dejected silence as the enormity of what their failure meant to the worlds that she had known and loved sank deep into her consciousness.

"Now, now my sweet girl," Ahriman cooed seductively in Hanna's ear, as he ran his long, delicate fingers under her chin to lift her swollen eyes to his. "This is no time for tears. This is an occasion of great joy! For mankind will soon be on the road to a much better, more dignified future. A posterity which has been denied to him for far too long by your lascivious Elder Gods, smitten by their carnal desires, who have enslaved mankind to their crass prurience."

Hanna looked up into the deep indigo-blue eyes of the Supreme Lord of Darkness, they were unexpectedly kind, further throwing her mind into a state of confusion. His prominent forehead had an ever so slight depression in the skull bone that looked tender, as if it had not yet completely healed. She looked at his face, which retained a youthful splendor despite being horrifically scarred all along the left side from the assassination attempt on his life. Ahriman's left eyelid and the left side of his mouth also drooped noticeably, giving him the appearance of one who has had a stroke or suffers from Bell's palsy. And yet, despite all the depravity that Ahriman was guilty of and the suffering he had inflicted upon mankind since its creation, Hanna was surprised that she was unable to feel hatred for him even though she knew that his triumph meant the total obliteration of everything that she held sacred. Her overwhelming emotion, staring into the face of purest evil, was one of abject pity. Pity…for those poor mortals whose lives would be forever changed by Ahriman's triumph.

Pity...for the Elder Gods who would have no safe haven in which to hide from Ahriman's energized forces. Pity...for Rocky who must be suffering excruciating pain from his wound. Pity...for Aaron, poor brave Aaron, whose one desire was to avenge the death of his beloved Khydyra. And lastly, pity for herself, for her weakness at not being able to either save her friends or fulfill the trust that had been placed upon her by the Elder Gods.

Ahriman gently placed his hand under Hanna's arm and lifted her to her feet.

"Come my sweet, a new day is dawning and I want to personally show it to you."

Hanna did not resist. How could she, she wondered to herself. Ahriman was a giant, much taller than any of the Archons or other Princes of Hell by a good 2 meters. And he was an Archangel, second only to God in his power and potency...though with his impending victory, perhaps now more powerful than even the King of Heaven. She and her compatriots had come to stop his forces from breaching the Gates between the Worlds...not to kill the Great Satan himself, whom they had always assumed was already dead. Seeing him alive was beyond anything that they had prepared for. It would have taken much greater preparation and all of their collective power to destroy him in the sanctity of his own lair, surrounded as he was by his Imperial Guards and his Princes of Hell. Looking back at the series of events that they had experienced since their ragged caravan had neared the outskirts of Ba'ir, Hanna quite frankly was willing to concede that perhaps the power of Ahriman had been working in the background all along, leading them like a siren's call to just this final defeat. She sighed heavily, as Ahriman brought her to the foot of the High Altar.

"Now, wait here, my sweet," he said quietly, "The time has come to usher in our new world order." Ahriman smiled a beatific grin and then turned to mount the stairs to the upper level of the altar.

Hanna followed him with her eyes as Ornias and the rest of the high ranking Princes in the Great Lord's retinue closed ranks about her. She gazed at Ahriman's strong, muscular flanks, so cut and defined, covered in a thick matting of golden brown hair, and then followed their sinewy line up his sleek, toned and almost hairless torso, noting the huge, jagged scar which ran from under his right armpit all the way down to his slender waist, blazing a fiery crimson against his alabaster skin. Taking in the totality of his magnificent body and the dramatic flaring of his huge wings as he stood under the ornately carved bronze canopy of the Baldacchino, Hanna almost fell over in shock when she glimpsed a familiar figure crouched high in the uppermost rafters of the canopy, directly above the Great Lord.

"Hey Beautiful, miss me?"

Using their special frequency, Antipas Pergamos seemed to be in a ridiculously jolly mood. Hanna was instantly pissed. Had he been there all along, while she and the others had been fighting for their lives against the onslaught of hellfire that had trapped them in the Confessio? Why hadn't he tried to help them? He was an eleventh-degree Master Adept of the Ordo Templi Orientis, for crying out loud! That potent magick is precisely why PsyOps wanted him on this mission! He was supposed to be the indispensable difference between salvation or the enslavement of mankind!

"Ah, don't be mad at me, Beautiful," Antipas playfully cajoled. "I only just got here. And besides, suicide missions aren't really my style."

"*DAMN YOU*, Tip!" Hanna replied sharply, barely concealing her emotions from those around her.

Antipas put a finger to his lips.

"Shhhh! You don't want to ruin this last little bit of magick, now, do you? After all, I didn't ask to be a part of all of this drama. Y*ou*, Rocky, Gabriella and the rest of that heathen PsyOps crew forced me into this mess to save *your* sorry asses, not to mention the whole of Creation to boot, from Ahriman and His hordes, remember? So… that's what I'm going to do, Beautiful. I *always* keep up my end of things, even though I can't vouch the same for any of the other signatories. Trust me, my beloved Mistress, you're going to owe me *BIG* time!"

Ahriman, standing on the raised platform of the High Altar, which made even his gargantuan form seem small amidst the grandeur of the Great Hall of Hell, began a long, monotonous chant that started in the very depths of his sonorous bass and rose in intensity until the domes vaulting the nave were vibrating with the sound of his voice. Hanna felt the pit of her stomach rumbling in sync with his chanting. The force of it welled up through her body and she felt as if the breath was being crushed out of her chest. She realized that Ahriman was drawing energy from all those in the Great Hall, using their life force to infinitely multiply his own supernatural omnipotence to take on the characteristics of a true God. The psychic power being concentrated in his body was unimaginable, and if he continued Hanna worried, he might actually drain so much life force that everyone in the Great Hall could die. Panicked by this new terrible possibility, Hanna quickly looked up at Antipas, still hiding in the rafters. She hadn't noticed that she was being intently watched the whole time and when she made the sharp movement of her chin toward the top of the Baldacchino, Ornias immediately saw Antipas shifting his position up in the cupola.

"INFIDEL!!!" Ornias screamed at the top of his lungs.

In an instant a thousand bolts of lightening were sent hurtling toward the top of the cupola from every member of the Imperial Guard. Ahriman, deep in his trance, barely registered the interruption. He opened his eyes for a brief second and looked up above into the recesses of the cupola just as first volleys struck. He glimpsed a sight that so surprised him that he didn't even have time to react before the whole top of the cupola exploded into a cloud of dust from the terrific impact of the force directed at it. Shards of shattered metal and splinters of gold, silver and platinum showered down on the Great Lord, his wings still outstretched. The Imperial Guard rushed forward to form a picket encircling Ahriman, their weapons raised and pointing outward, away from their Great Lord. Raising his hand like a patient father bringing order out of the chaos, The Great Lord smiled as a hush spread throughout the expanse of the Great Hall. In a calm voice, as if nothing had happened, Ahriman resumed his chant with renewed vigor. As the intensity of the vibration reached its zenith, the whole nave filled with the light of a million suns, bathing everything in an immaculate golden glow. Hanna thought it was as if the whole top of the Great Hall had been lifted up from its foundations and catapulted through the living rock into the world of the living, heralding the dawn of the Age of the Great Satan. Even the air in the nave felt different...smelled sweeter than the fetid stench that normally filled the realms of darkness. Hanna knew from that sweet smell that the armies of Ahriman had breached the final Gates and now walked freely upon the surface of the Earth. Amidst the ensuing cheers and shouts from the multitude of demons in the nave, she began to cry.

"Don't cry, Beautiful," The Great Lord called out to her softly, in that rumbling bass of his. "It's a new day dawning, filled with endless possibilities! Come! The fun is just beginning!"

Hanna was more than a little stunned by his choice of words and she looked sharply at him. Ahriman returned her gaze, a twinkle in his eyes that wasn't there before. She tilted her head, puzzled. His face was…different…somehow. There was absolutely no sign of the palsy that had seemed to paralyze his face before. And there was a very definite energetic shift in the aura of the Great Satan. He seemed to be enjoying himself immensely, as if the imminent triumph of his armies had enervated and rejuvenated him. In the far, distant reaches of her mind's eye, Hanna tried to make sense of it all…especially a disturbing shadow of memory that seemed, improbably, to reflect something that had happened in the merest fraction of a second before the cupola of the Baldacchino was vaporized by the lightening bolts. Hanna had to keep shaking her head, trying to get the incredible specter to crystalize but it just wouldn't fully clarify itself. Could it be? She wondered. Had she actually seen what her mind thought she saw? It was just too fantastical, too outrageous for it to be real. Had she just witnessed Antipas Pergamos taking the immortal soul of Ahriman the Great Satan? Hanna shook her head yet again as the denizens of Hell yelped and clapped and shouted at the top of their lungs in celebration of their Great Lord and the beginning of His reign on earth. She stared once more into the face of the Great Satan. He winked at her and then raised his arms in triumph over his head before leading his Imperial Guards down the main aisle of the Great Hall and into His new domains.

Hanna shook her head yet again. As she was being lead out of the Great Hall by one of the Imperial Guards, she caught only a fleeting glimpse of Ornias, the Archangel closest to the Great Satan. He, too, wore a puzzled expression on his face. He caught her eye briefly. Then dismissed whatever wavering thoughts still clouded his mind and resolutely strode after his Supreme Lord.

* * *

ABOUT WM KANE

Wm Kane is an African-American author of novellas that pack a big punch. Dealing with themes that focus on the existential human questions of the meaning of this Life, Religion and Man's relationship with his fellow Man (in the meta sense...so women are also included!), Kane's works of fiction, fantasy, sci-fi take readers on compelling, fast-paced journeys, filled with unique characters, exotic settings, lots of intrigue, unexpected twists and surprise endings, all while conveying a message of hope, possibility and faith in the triumph of Good over Evil. Most of all, Kane endeavors to populate his worlds with a multicultural cast of folks drawn from his real life encounters and experiences, ranging from the down-right straight-up sexy as *Hell* to the boy (or girl) next door...sometimes gay, sometimes straight, sometimes in-between...but always in 'yo face, with a point of view that demands to be heard and a heart of pure gold.

His most recent novella, MEMOIR OF A TIME YET TO COME, was published in 2012 and is available on all ebook platforms, including Amazon, Barnes & Noble, Smashwords, iBookStore and KoboBooks.